HER FOUR-YEAR BABY SECRET

CHAPTER ONE

ANOTHER ghost, that's all it was.

Paramedic Fiona Murchison jerked the ambulance into a lower gear and the heavy vehicle skidded a little on the steep gravel surface of the mountain road.

'Whoa!' Her partner, Shane, grinned. 'Thought we were covering this rally, not competing in it!'

Fiona chuckled. 'Just you wait. I might try a Scandinavian flick on the next corner.'

'A what?'

'It's a turning technique. You steer a bit into the opposite direction of the turn and put your foot on the accelerator and brake at the same time. That makes you slide away from the turn and then you change the steering, release the brake and keep your foot on the accelerator, and you sort of slingshot your way around the corner in the direction you want to go.'

Shane eyed the steep drop on his side of the road nervously. 'A little knowledge can be a dangerous thing, Fi.'

'Don't worry. We're not going much further. Just up to the spectator area for all those people who've been keen enough to hike up the track.'

'There's a lot of them.'

'Yeah.' Fiona turned her head briefly, surprised by the steady queue of climbers. 'And there must be a couple of thousand at the bottom. It's a popular event.'

So many people. It was no wonder her ghost had made an appearance. Given the sheer numbers and the fact that males were more drawn to watching motor sports, there would have to be hundreds enough above average height to stand out in the crowd. Dark, floppy hair wasn't that uncommon either and more than a few men had that arrogant way of walking—as though the world was their personal playground.

'I guess your Sam is here somewhere?'

'Of course. With my mum. He wanted to stay near the flags.'

'I'll bet he's excited.'

'Over the moon.'

Shane chuckled. 'Like every four-year-old boy here, I expect, getting up close and personal to this kind of action.'

'Yeah.' Fiona eased the ambulance towards the official tents marking the relatively level area that gave a vantage point to see the road as it continued to snake up the mountainside towards a ski-field that wouldn't have snow for some weeks yet. 'I reckon it's more than that with Sam, though. It's definitely in the blood.'

'Did he see his dad race, then, when he was a baby?'

'No.' Fiona switched off the engine and unclipped her safety belt. 'I didn't even know I was pregnant at Al's funeral. I had so much going on with Dad having another stroke and deciding to come home to New Zealand that I was four months down the track before I put two and two together.'

'You OK?' Shane might be a junior ambulance officer but he wasn't short on compassion. 'This can't be easy for you.'

'It's five years since Al was killed and the accident was at a rally in Switzerland, not Queenstown.'

'Still…'

Fiona shrugged. 'I can deal with it.'

It was easier up the hillside a bit. Away from the buzz of the flagged area where the bright cars and the stars of the sport were surrounded by their support teams and fans. Funny how it had been the sight of a random spectator in the crowd, rather than one of the superstars, that had conjured up the ghost. The intensity of that nasty lurch was fading now. Fiona could look down at the colourful scene below and feel nothing more than a kind of nostalgia.

No. Relief, actually, that she was no longer a part of that world. She hoped the passion for this kind of drama wasn't really running through the blood of her son. The kind of life it could produce wasn't what she'd wish for Sam. It might be dramatic and exciting and potentially rewarding but it wasn't…*real.*

This was real. The stark beauty of the rugged mountain peaks of the Remarkables making a forbidding silhouette against a sky as blue as only Central Otago could boast. The surprising warmth of the autumn sunshine. And, best of all, the knowledge that a small, dark-haired boy was not too far away, probably clutching more than one of his precious collection of rally car models. His eyes would be shining and anyone lucky enough to be close would find their world a little brighter by seeing his grin. A happy, safe little boy who was protected by two women who loved him to bits.

Fiona knew her mother would have taken her warning on board to keep a low profile. She didn't want the media discovering that Alistair Stewart's son was here. Didn't want the perfect life she had spent years building for them disrupted by the havoc she knew the media could create.

The reasonably level area the ambulance was in—a good kilometre uphill from the start flags—was awash with caravans and tents, spectators and officials. A helicopter hovered overhead, ready to film the event, but the sound of engines revving and people shouting still drifted up from below.

The qualifying heats had finished and the main event was due to begin where one car at a time would tackle the steep grades and nearly a hundred turns on the twelve-kilometre track, many of them impossible-looking hairpin corners with only a low metal barricade on the drop side. The team with the shortest time would win and the buzz of expectation was steadily rising.

Even Fiona was catching it. Like a sensory ghost, it was creeping in on her. The sounds of the engines and the excited shouting and laughter. The gasps of admiration or horror as vehicles were tested to their limits. The smell of petrol and the dust the cars raised as they hurtled past. The bright colours of the cars with their sponsors' logos, often with matching helmets and suits for the drivers. Any one of those figures in the distance could have been Al and a close-up, albeit brief, flash of a face grim with concentration going past the ambulance position and into a tight turn gave Fi just as much of a lurch as that figure in the crowd had done.

Thankfully, her senses became almost immune after the first hour or so and Fiona was able to relax a little. Enjoy it, even.

'That's called "yumping",' she told Shane, pointing up the hill to where a car had become airborne after a sharp dip and then rise in the road. 'They flick the steering a tad in mid-air to try and land one wheel at a time and spread the load of the impact.'

'Ever tried it yourself?'

'Only once and that was enough. Al's parents had this huge country property in England and there was a practice course out the back.'

'Wow!'

'His dad was a Warbirds fanatic. He had a collection of World War Two planes and even had his own airfield there as well.'

'Adventurous family.'

'Too adventurous. His parents were killed in a plane crash a year before Al had his accident. A new Spitfire or something he'd added to his collection that had some massive engine failure on its first trial run.'

'Good grief! So the whole family wiped themselves out with adventure sports?'

'Almost. Al had a brother who was about ten years younger than him and was the black sheep of the family, I guess. He went to med school. Mind you, I suppose he had a few of the genes because he went off to join Médecins sans Frontières not long after his parents' funeral and I haven't seen or heard from him since, and that's sad because Sam would so love to have a *real* uncle.'

Any wistful note in Fiona's voice was lost on Shane, who didn't seem to be listening any more. He had sucked in his breath at the new cloud of dust obscuring the car still hurtling downhill. 'This guy is *moving*!'

'Must be one of the last competitors. He knows what kind of time he has to beat.'

Shane shook his head. 'Don't fancy his chances if he misses a turn.'

'Could be quite a scramble for us, that's for sure.' Fiona grinned. 'If we have to go mountain climbing, you get to carry the gear, mate.'

The car roared closer. Into the tight turn nearest their parking area. Another glimpse of two grim faces. Another cloud of dust and then…

Then that kind of frozen moment in time that sheer horror could produce as the car failed to correct its turn, continuing to skid at high speed through the barrier, which failed to slow the huge missile in any way. Straight towards the crowd of spectators.

The driver must have tried desperately to avert disaster. Maybe he wrenched the steering-wheel hard enough to cause the flip and roll of the vehicle. People were screaming. Trying to hurl themselves out of its path. But some were clearly failing, being clipped by the car and thrown for some distance before hitting the ground.

The finale came only seconds after the drama had begun, with the car slamming into the back of a caravan selling hot dogs and ice cream. A cloud of black smoke billowed and then the ominous lick of flames appeared.

Fiona shook the numbing horror from her brain. She was the senior medical officer on scene and she had to act on the training she had received in dealing with a multi-casualty incident. She grabbed the portable radio hanging behind the driver's seat and a fluorescent vest from a hook beside it. Then she headed for the stunned-looking group of race officials in that split second after the car had finally stopped its journey of destruction.

Two more officials appeared from a tent, carrying fire extinguishers, and ran towards the car. Many of the crowd were still running for safety, some carrying children, but others were turning back in response to cries from the injured, milling helplessly and beginning to obscure Fiona's view of the scene as she tried to assess the kind of numbers they were dealing with.

She had her finger on the 'Push To Talk' button of the radio.

'We have a code five hundred,' she informed the central communications centre. 'Multi-casualty. Possibly twenty victims. Status still unknown.'

The two ambulances from the main area at the start and finish flags were already on the move, starting the slow climb up the gravel road. A Red Cross Jeep was ahead of them, dust billowing from beneath its wheels.

'Rescue helicopter back-up needed,' Fiona told Control. 'I'll get back to you as soon as we've triaged.'

She turned to the people around her. 'Shane, grab my kit and some triage labels.'

Fiona pointed to an official holding a megaphone. 'Direct any uninjured people to clear the scene. Any injured people capable of walking are to go to the administration tent. I'm going to assess what we have left.'

'What about the guys in the car?'

Fiona took a quick glance over her shoulder as Shane came running back. 'Make sure the fire is out and then see if they're trapped. We may need the fire service up here as well.'

Shrugging on the jerkin that designated her as scene commander, Fiona moved to triage the victims into a priority treatment queue but she couldn't lose sight of the incident as a whole.

'Send any new ambulance crews to report to me as they arrive,' she told another official. 'And put out a call over the main PA system for anyone with medical training that can assist.'

It was too easy for medics to go towards the first injured person they could see and then get caught up with the assessment and treatment while someone with more life-threatening injuries lay unattended nearby. Fiona's task right now was to look at everybody and grade the severity of their conditions. Basic treatment, like opening an airway or controlling a severe haemorrhage, could be done but no more until everybody had been seen.

Just repositioning an unconscious person so that their airway was no longer occluded could save a life—but not unless it happened within a short space of time and, given the number of bodies still lying on the ground as the mobile people responded to the official's orders to move towards the tent and clear the scene, she was going to have to move fast.

It was hard, ignoring the cries of pain or screams for help.

'My leg! I can't move!'

'It *hurts*...'

'Help! Please, help!'

The people calling were conscious. Their airways and breathing were clear enough for speech so they weren't going to be the first priority.

Except for the one Fiona and Shane came to first.

'Please, help,' the man said again, 'It's my wife. I...' His voice choked. 'I couldn't get to her to pull her away... And the car...'

'Okay.' Fiona crouched beside the motionless figure of the woman. A trickle of blood could be seen from her nose. There was a smear of blood on one ear but Fiona couldn't take the time to check whether it was external or, more ominously, the result of an internal head injury. The woman was breathing and the only blood loss obvious was a wound on the back of her head. Fiona ripped open a dressing and covered the wound.

'Stay here with her,' she directed the husband. 'Talk to her. Hold her head—like this...' She positioned his hands.

'Keep her as still as you can if she starts to wake up. Someone will be here very soon to put a collar on and assess her properly.' Fiona turned to Shane. 'Pink label,' she said.

'What's that for?' the husband asked anxiously as Shane slipped the rubber band of the label around the woman's wrist.

'It tells the treatment crews who needs attention first,' Fiona explained as they moved towards the next victim only thirty seconds after stopping. 'Pink is top of the list.'

The next person, only a few metres away, had torn clothing and flesh on his left side that looked more like a glancing blow from the runaway vehicle than impact with the ground. The man was conscious and breathing but his speech was incoherent between groans of agony.

'Unstable pelvis,' Fiona said grimly, seconds later. 'Pink label.' He could have other serious internal injuries but a fractured pelvis alone could be enough to cause catastrophic blood loss.

A child was screaming, both arms held in the air with the hands drooping at odd angles.

'Help him,' his mother demanded, catching Fiona's arm as she walked rapidly in their direction.

'He'll be seen very soon,' Fiona assured her. 'Take him to the tent.'

'No! *Wait!*'

But Fiona and Shane kept moving. Anyone that could stand up and scream as loudly as that boy had an excellent airway and level of consciousness. Not that Fiona didn't have every sympathy for the mother. Running at a level just below her need to handle this situation to the best of her professional ability was a very real horror that her son could be involved.

What if they hadn't stayed near the finish flags?

Fiona couldn't afford to distracted by what was probably an imaginary fear—there were no other children to be seen among the injured after all—but as soon as she had even a second to spare, she would be calling her mother for reassurance.

A second ambulance crew intercepted their path.

'Take the woman over there,' Fiona directed. 'Unconscious. Pink label. Head injury. Put a collar on and start oxygen. OP airway if her GCS is still less than ten. Do a secondary survey. Someone will be there to establish IV access as soon as possible.'

She was already crouching in front of a dazed-looking man who was sitting, staring at his hands.

'Oh, my God…' he kept saying between frantic gulps of air.

'It's OK,' Fiona told him. 'Try and slow your breathing down. Are you asthmatic?'

He didn't seem to hear her. 'Oh, my God,' he said again. 'I was holding my camera… It got caught on the car…'

A strap had probably been caught around his fingers. The index finger was obviously dislocated and probably broken. The middle finger had been ripped cleanly off the hand. Typically, the traumatic amputation had caused blood vessels to close off completely and the wound was barely bleeding.

'Green label,' Fiona directed Shane. 'Get someone to take him to the tent. He's got a bit of a wheeze. They'll need to check if he's an asthmatic and give him some salbutamol if it gets any worse.'

The fleeting glance she took around them at the litter of abandoned personal belongings, many of which were spattered with blood or covered with dust, confirmed the futility of anyone taking the time to try and find the missing finger. With lives potentially being lost around them, it had to be rated well down any priority list. Fiona hurried towards the next victim. An update to the control centre would need to be made soon.

She needed back-up. Preferably highly skilled.

Nick Stewart heard the call for medical assistance over the PA system but he was already moving back up the track, having heard the crash and then the screams of the injured.

Why had he decided to go down to the finish flags to watch the last competitor make it home?

Why had he come here at all when he had known how many ghosts would be in evidence?

Here he was, a newcomer to a tiny country at the bottom of the world, finally ready to stop running and try to build a life that was grounded and real. And on his first full day he had chosen to resurrect memories that were among the most painful he had.

Which was why he had come, of course. Nick pushed himself up the steep track at a speed that was making his muscles ache and his lungs burn. If there was a challenge that had to be faced, Nick Stewart faced it. If the obstacle seemed insurmountable, he found a way to break through it. The ghosts had been held at bay until now because there had been no reason to lay them but if he was serious about a new start, he wasn't going to allow himself to back down from what needed to be dealt with.

Two ambulances and a Red Cross vehicle had gone well past him now. He should have flagged one down. Told the crews that he was an emergency physician—fresh out of dealing with mass casualty incidents in war zones—and that he had practising privileges in New Zealand because he was the locum for their community hospital for the next month.

He was too used to relying on his own resources, that was the problem. He'd turned and legged it towards the track he had just come down as soon as he had heard the crash and now he was going to be several minutes behind the play by the time he reached the scene, dammit! His mission of getting uphill was being further hampered by the flow of people being herded away from the scene. Shocked-looking people, who kept slowing and turning to look behind them as though they still couldn't believe what they'd seen.

Hopefully, there were some competent paramedics among the crews on those emergency vehicles, but this was rural New Zealand. A disaster like this was probably a once-in-a-lifetime event for these people and, no matter how highly trained they were, nothing really counted like experience.

The small crowd of people in the largest tent all seemed to have suffered relatively minor injuries. A loud woman was demanding attention, her hands on the shoulders of a young child who had clearly broken both his arms. Some of the group were sporting large green tags on their wrists and Nick recognised the triage labels with an inward nod of approval. Someone here knew what they were doing.

He approached a man wearing a race official's vest. 'I'm a doctor,' he said crisply. 'You were calling for assistance. Who's in charge here?'

'Outside,' the official directed. 'Find the medic wearing a vest that says "Scene Commander".'

That particular vest was not immediately obvious but there were at least half a dozen people wearing the uniforms of ambulance officers, moving among blanket-wrapped victims lying on the ground. Uninjured people boosted the numbers. Nick passed a man who was holding the head of an unconscious woman as an ambulance officer slipped a stiff neck collar into position. She had a pink label on her wrist.

'I'm a doctor,' Nick said again. 'Your patient breathing OK?'

A second ambulance officer, holding a portable gas cylinder and mask, nodded. 'We'll get oxygen on as soon she's collared.'

'GCS?'

'She's been moving a bit and wouldn't tolerate an airway. Maybe 11?'

Nick nodded. There could well be people that needed his attention more and, besides, he had a responsibility to report to whoever was in charge of this rescue scene. The success of managing a large-scale disaster depended on the chain of command, good communication and the best use of all possible resources. Mavericks who did their own thing were a liability and what good would he be anyway, without anything more than the most basic equipment?

'Where's your scene commander?'

'Over there.' The tubing of the mask uncoiled as the ambulance officer pointed.

Nick passed the wreck of the car wedged against the hot-dog caravan. The group of men—some still holding fire extinguishers, others trying to open the jammed doors—obscured his view of what might be inside. His brisk stride faltered for a second.

Could he face his worst demon and attend the occupants of this vehicle? Step back in time to when he'd lost not only his childhood hero but the last living member of his family?

Yes…of course he could.

He reached the side of the car just as one of the jammed doors was prised open. The words 'I'm a doctor' cleared a space for him instantly.

Two men were inside, both conscious and distressed and talking in what sounded like a European language. They were both breathing without difficulty, had strong pulses and there was no sign of obvious bleeding. One of the men had burns to his face but they weren't serious and Nick couldn't see any singed hair or soot inside his nostrils, which might indicate respiratory tract involvement. He knew how to undo the harnesses and could check cervical spines and then chests for any major trauma.

'Nothing life threatening,' he said to the officials. 'The front of the car is buckled enough to trap them. Is the fire completely out?'

'Seems to be.'

'You'll need cutting gear to get them free. They'll be OK till then. A cold, wet cloth on the driver's face would be helpful. I need to find the scene commander for the medics.'

'Over there, mate.'

Yes. Nick could see the vest with the correct designation. On a slight figure who was crouched beside a body. A female, obviously, given the long braid of dark hair hanging between her shoulder blades.

'Pink label,' he heard her instruct the man beside her. 'And I'm not happy with his breathing. This one's top of the list for intubation. How many more for triage can you see, Shane?'

Her partner was scanning the area. 'I think this is the last, apart from the guys in the car.'

'Great. We'll stay here for the moment, then. I've just got to update Control.' She stood up, unclipping a hand-held radio from her belt.

'I'm a doctor,' Nick said to her back. 'Emergency physician. Where do you need me first?'

'Right here.' The woman turned. 'Status-one patient. Chest injuries…' Her voice trailed into silence. 'Oh, my God,' she breathed a moment later. *'Nick?'*

He'd know who she was the moment she'd turned. Before that even, from the tone of her voice or that lithe movement when she'd stood up when long limbs had moved with all the grace of a dancer.

But, then, he'd often seen a similar movement or long, curly dark hair or heard something in a voice or seen it in a smile that had reminded him of Fi, hadn't he? He'd spent years experiencing the jolt of a missed heartbeat or a catch of his breath only to find it had been just the whisper of a ghost.

So much time had passed since he'd actually seen Fi and this was unexpected enough to be mind-blowing. He had assumed she was still a nurse in a London hospital somewhere. What the hell was she doing, being a para-medic, let alone being in charge of a disaster scene on a mountain in what was the back of beyond in international terms? Was this why those letters had been returned unopened?

In its own way, this was as shocking as being plunged into managing a disaster scene. Fiona's brain whirled at light-ning speed in the second or two she simply stared at Nick.

Why was it so shocking? If she had ever been going to meet her ex-brother-in-law, the venue of a top-level rally car competition was the obvious setting. Events like this were far more part of Nick's personal history than her own.

Given that her adrenaline levels were at an all-time high, coping with the equally unexpected, large-scale disaster, coming face to face with Nick Stewart should barely have registered, let alone be giving her this moment of utter confusion.

Fiona wanted to throw her arms around this man. To hug him and tell him how wonderful it was to see him again.

But she also wanted to plant her hands on his chest. To shove him away as hard as she could. To make the accusations that, even as recently as her conversation with Shane just before all this had begun, still echoed in the back of her mind.

The anger was still there.

Maybe it was lucky there was no way Fiona could take even another millisecond to choose between the conflicting reactions. With a deliberate mental shake, she banished anything remotely personal. Instead, she allowed herself a wash of relief that somebody more qualified that she was could share the responsibility of caring for all these injured people. Someone that she knew could be trusted to handle anything that could prove too much of a challenge.

Astonishing how that gave her a new kind of strength. She *could* cope with this—the biggest incident she had ever faced. She would do her job and do it well.

'My kit's here,' she told Nick crisply. 'It should have everything you need. My partner Shane will help you.' She turned her back, pushed the button on the radio and began to walk away.

'Three status-one patients,' she informed Control. 'Four status two, six status three so far. What's the ETA for the rescue helicopter?'

CHAPTER TWO

'IS THERE a stethoscope in that kit?'

'Yep.' Shane crouched to flip the catches open. He handed the instrument to Nick and then fished in his pocket. 'You want some gloves?'

'Thanks. Can you expose the chest for me, please?'

Nick pulled on the latex gloves as Shane used shears to cut the clothing so that they could examine their patient effectively. He took just one more, semi-stunned glance at the retreating figure of Fiona.

'You guys local?' he asked Shane. With an event this size, extra cover could well have been pulled in from some distance away.

Shane nodded, cutting through the last section of a woollen jersey and the shirt beneath. Nick unconsciously echoed the nod as he fitted the earpieces of the stethoscope into place, tucking away the satisfying information that he was going to be able to talk to Fi properly when this was over and then transferring his total concentration to watching their patient's efforts to breathe.

'Asymmetrical chest wall,' he noted. 'And paradoxical movement.' The disc of the stethoscope dangled for a few more seconds as Nick laid his hands on the damaged chest.

'Flail chest?' Shane queried.

'Yeah. Let's get some high-flow oxygen going and use a bag mask to provide some positive pressure ventilation.' Nick listened carefully with the stethoscope to gauge air entry as Shane connected the oxygen and started the flow.

'Absent breath sounds on the left side,' he said tersely. 'Do you carry a needle decompression kit?'

'Here.' Shane handed him the package and then reached for an alcohol wipe to clean the skin.

'Thanks.' Nick caught the younger man's gaze for a moment, to communicate the fact that he was impressed. 'Exactly the right spot. You know what you're doing, don't you?'

Shane's smile was fleeting. The next few seconds were tense as Nick inserted the needle to allow the air trapped outside the lung in their patient's chest cavity to escape. The hiss of air was lost in the noise around them but the man's breathing improved almost instantly.

Nick took a deeper breath himself. 'Let's get some baseline vitals and IV access. Fi's right—this chap needs intubation.'

As they worked to try and stabilise the man for the next few minutes, Nick became aware of the change in command taking place around them. The police were now in charge, as they should be, to allow medical personnel like Fiona to do what they did best and care for the injured. He could see her doing just that, only a few metres away from his own position.

She had a race official holding a bag of IV fluid aloft and she was uncoiling the tubing of a giving set to attach it to the line she must have already secured in her patient's arm. She was clearly intent on her task but at precisely the moment Nick's gaze rested on Fiona, she glanced up.

For just a split second, their gazes caught. A fraction of a moment completely inconsequential in the general level of urgency and stress but it felt curiously longer. And more personal. Almost like a physical touch.

The connection was still there, wasn't it? Shockingly so, given the space of time since they'd last seen each other, but, then, this had been so unexpected.

Disturbing…

Nick's gaze shifted virtually instantly. He could see Red Cross personnel setting up a treatment area in the largest tent available as the people with less serious injuries were checked and moved elsewhere. A helicopter was landing, unloading people and equipment, presumably from the local hospital.

That was where he should be, even though he wasn't officially due to start work until next week. This was frustrating, not having a handle on what resources were available in the way of staff and theatre facilities or even what the transport times to the nearest base hospitals would be.

Two first-aid volunteers were pushing a stretcher, with a bright orange backboard on the top, over the rough ground. They came in Nick's direction.

'Pink label,' one of them noted. 'Fi said to go to those first.'

They veered closer. 'The tent's ready,' the other told Nick. 'You want to move your patient inside?'

Nick looked up from where he had unrolled the intubation kit to check its contents. People were carrying equipment like blankets and IV fluids into the tent. He could see bright lights on inside.

This patient was seriously injured. With a flail chest, there were two or more ribs broken in two or more places, which meant he had sustained a significant blunt chest injury. He was at risk of lung contusion, further deterioration of his breathing due to air or blood in the chest cavity, brain damage from lack of oxygen or going into shock from blood loss. He could well have associated injuries to his thoracic spine, a diaphragmatic tear or even a cardiac injury.

Until they could get this man to an emergency department, possibly Theatre and then an intensive care unit, all they could do was maintain his level of oxygenation by supporting ventilation. Intubation and manual ventilation would be much easier to manage in the relatively controlled space of the tent.

'We need the backboard,' Nick told the stretcher crew. 'And a couple more people to help with a log roll. Shane, can you support his neck and keep the oxygen on?'

'Sure.'

Another stretcher was being carried into the tent in front of Nick's patient. Fiona had a bag of IV fluid in her hand as she walked beside it. A second bag was now being held by a police officer.

'Rescue helicopter is due any minute,' she informed Nick. 'We'll evacuate two of the status-one patients as long as they're stable.'

'This guy won't be stable until I've intubated,' Nick responded. 'I've done a needle decompression for a pneumothorax but his breathing's still inadequate.'

Fiona held his gaze and this time it didn't create those disturbing ripples. This was a professional discussion and, maybe for the first time, they were on an equal footing. In this situation they had the same skills and the same goals. The only real difference was in the amount of experience clocked up.

'You OK with Shane to assist you?'

What would she say if he said he wasn't? Would Fi offer

to assist him herself? That odd feeling in his gut returned. Maybe he wasn't ready to work quite that closely with this woman. What Nick really needed was just a few minutes to himself to get his head around this and that wasn't going to be possible in the near future. Besides, Shane had already demonstrated his capabilities as an assistant.

'Sure,' he told Fiona. 'More than OK.'

His confidence was not misplaced. Without being asked, the junior paramedic folded a towel to the thickness needed to provide the ideal 'sniffing' position of their patient's head. He pre-oxygenated while Nick readied the laryngoscope and endotracheal tube and his hand moved to supply cricoid pressure at precisely the moment needed.

'Good job,' Nick told him. 'You could be doing this yourself, I think.'

'Nah.' Shane shook his head as he squeezed the bag mask while Nick listened to the chest to confirm correct placement of the tube. 'I'm not qualified yet. Fi's got me into a training programme, though, and she's the best teacher.'

'Mmm.' A flash of memory came unbidden to a corner of Nick's mind as he attended to the automatic task of slipping a bite block between their patient's teeth and securing the tube protecting his airway.

He'd been studying for an exam. With so much going on at home it hadn't been an easy task. The party to celebrate his older brother's engagement had lasted the whole weekend and it hadn't helped that Al had, once again, hit the jackpot.

He'd found the perfect woman.

Fiona had heard his frustrated sigh as she'd passed the library door. She had given the impression that an excuse to escape the revelry had been more than welcome. She'd been so interested in what he had been studying and had sympathised with the scramble his brain had been in, trying to memorise medical terms that had seemed far too similar.

'Give us your pen,' Fiona had instructed. 'And some paper. Look...' A diagram had taken shape. 'Glucose that's not needed for energy gets stored as glycogen in the liver and muscle cells. That's glycogenesis. When it's needed again, it gets split up. That's glycogenolysis...'

Twenty minutes later Nick had found the whole physiological picture of diabetes perfectly clear. He'd never forgotten that lesson. The soft, melodious sound of Fi's voice with the curious accent that had been new for him, the ability to make things simple and the patience to make sure they were understood. The way she'd used her hands as an extension of her voice or to tuck a wayward curl behind her ear when she'd bent forward to write or draw.

Yes. Fiona had been a great teacher all those years ago. She was probably brilliant now, with the addition of maturity and experience. Shane was lucky. The thought made a curious sensation needle Nick. It if wasn't so ridiculous, he might have labelled it jealousy.

Threading the soft tape under the man's neck, Nick tied it to the other side of the device intended to keep the tube securely in place. Shane helped to slide a cervical neck collar into place. Nick couldn't quite shake that odd feeling of envy.

'How long has Fiona been working here?'

'Only two years, full time. She started as a volunteer but then Maggie got pregnant and persuaded her to cross-credit her nursing qualifications and then go further. She wanted Fi to take over so she could be a full-time mother for a while.'

'Maggie?' The name was familiar.

'Patterson. She's married to Hugh who's the medical director of Lakeview Hospital.'

'Of course.' Nick hung a fresh bag of IV fluid, watching the oxygen saturation level on the monitor creep up to a far more acceptable level as Shane continued to assist their patient's respirations. Hugh Patterson was the doctor he was replacing for the next month so that he could travel for some post-graduate training.

'Patient status?' A police officer with a clipboard stepped close.

'Airway's secure and blood pressure's ninety over forty. Stable enough for transport, depending on how far he needs to go and who's travelling with him.'

'We've got a chopper ready to take two patients to Dunedin with an ICU doctor on board. There's another chopper due within fifteen minutes but it's smaller so it'll only take one.'

Fiona appeared from the bustle of people working around them. Her glance took in the intubation, the spinal immobilisation and the fluid replacement therapy under way. Her quick smile was both impressed and appreciative.

'You happy if we load your patient now, Nick? I've got a woman with a head injury going on the first chopper as well. There's a man with a fractured pelvis and abdominal injury in line for the second air evac if nobody else deteriorates in the meantime.'

'I'm happy,' Nick concurred. Actually, what he was experiencing in the wake of Fiona's approval went beyond a mundane 'happy'. How come he'd never had quite this level of satisfaction from impressing some of his senior colleagues in the last few years? He wanted to do more. 'Do you want me to travel with the second chopper?'

Fiona shook her head. 'There's someone coming for transit. I've got two people with moderate injuries in an ambulance to go down to Lakeview. Shane, could you drive, please?'

'Sure.'

'And, Nick, if you could go with them, it would be great. Hugh's at the hospital and he's called in one of the local GPs but when he heard you were here, he asked if you could come as well.'

'Of course. You going to manage here if I go now?'

Fiona gave a brief nod. 'We'll have the most critical patients evacuated very soon. We'll transport the others to Lakeview, including all the minors. There's a minibus on the way for them.'

He could see one of the passengers for the bus being escorted from the tent. A young man with a heavily bandaged hand. Fiona followed his gaze.

'Traumatic amputation of his middle finger,' she said. 'He's pretty upset. Set off a moderate asthma attack that needed treatment as well.' Her sigh encompassed sympathy for everybody who'd been involved in this incident. 'It'll be chaos down there for a while,' she added thoughtfully.

'Lakeview doesn't have surgical facilities, does it?'

'It's only set up for minor stuff but we've got a fixed-wing aircraft that can transport and we'll get the chopper back within a couple of hours if it's needed.'

Someone called her name and Fiona turned automatically. But then her head swung back to Nick.

'You'll be around for a while?' she queried. 'When this is over, I mean?'

Nick simply nodded. Would a month be long enough?

'Good.' With a frown, Fiona turned away again. 'We can talk later.'

A moment later, she was crouched by a different stretcher, a stethoscope in her hands as she reassessed a victim. That frown line was still creasing her forehead and while it was probably now due to concentration on the task at hand, Nick found he'd been left with the vaguely discomfiting notion that Fiona was not particularly looking forward to the opportunity to talk to him.

And why would she? His presence could only serve to remind her of what she'd lost. To challenge emotional scars that might have taken a very long time to heal. He would understand if that were the case. There was no denying that there were patches on his own soul feeling curiously raw thanks to this unexpected reunion.

Yes. He would understand. But even if his presence stirred up things that might best be forgotten, he was prepared to face this challenge. Maybe he needed to, in order to find closure.

The second helicopter arrived shortly after the ambulance driven by Shane started winding its way carefully down the shingle road. With the critical cases now evacuated and the people with obviously minor injuries climbing aboard the minibus, the scene was suddenly far less overwhelming.

Manageable, in fact.

The occupants of the rally car had been finally freed and, thanks to their harnesses, helmets and suits, they didn't appear to be badly injured. The co-driver had a possibly fractured ankle and the driver some first-degree burns to his face but no evidence of respiratory tract involvement. They were both Hungarian and the shock of what had happened made their English very difficult to follow. Their distress was all too obvious, however, and their signals made it clear that they wanted everybody else treated before receiving attention themselves.

'We need a translator,' Fiona told an official. 'Someone in their ground crew, perhaps.'

'Can you come over here?' A young police officer was waving at Fiona from the doorway of the tent.

She walked towards him. 'What's up?'

'There's a guy out here that doesn't seem to have much wrong with him but he's just sitting and isn't very co-operative. If he's just had too much to drink I can deal with him but I thought I'd better get you to check.'

'Good thinking.' Fiona approached the youth, who looked to be about eighteen.

'Go away,' he said loudly. 'Leave me alone.'

'Are you hurt?' Fiona was trying to assess him visually. He looked pale and the hair at his temples was damp, as though he'd been sweating. 'You haven't knocked your head, have you?'

'No. Go away.'

Fiona couldn't see any evidence of a head injury and she couldn't smell any alcohol. Then her gaze paused on the bony wrist protruding from a padded ski jacket.

'Just let me take your pulse and then I'll go away.' Fiona kept her tone reassuring and moved slowly as she crouched and gently captured his wrist. Having spotted the medic alert bracelet, she needed an opportunity to turn the disc over and read the inscription. 'What's your name?' she asked, both to try and start a conversation to assess level of consciousness and to distract the lad from what she was doing.

'What do you want to know for?' His glare was suspicious and the wrist Fiona was holding was attached to a tense fist. It could be jerked from her grasp at any moment and, given the level of combativeness being displayed, there was a distinct possibility the fist could head in the direction of Fiona's face. She held herself ready to dive for safety if necessary.

It wasn't the first time she had found herself in such a volatile situation. Most medics faced this kind of thing on occasion. Even if she hadn't had the shock of seeing Nick so unexpectedly today, she would probably—as she often had—remember him turning up to be the best man at his brother's wedding with a nasty, swollen black eye that he'd received from an emergency room patient suffering a lowered level of consciousness from a head injury.

She wasn't still thinking of him as she turned the bracelet over, however. Reading the designation of insulin-dependent diabetes mellitus dragged a corner of her brain back in time instantly. To when she'd found more in common with her future brother-in-law than an antipathy to being under a media spotlight.

Time with Nick that weekend had been an oasis in a totally new landscape for Fiona. A wildly exciting, irresistible landscape. But she had definitely needed the link to her old life. A chance to share knowledge from the career she loved.

Knowledge like the metabolic processes associated with glucose and the kind of symptoms produced when something was out of kilter. Symptoms like those of the young man sitting slumped in front of her right now.

'When did you last have something to eat?'

Her patient stared at her blankly.

'I need my kit,' Fiona told the police officer who was watching. 'Big grey box with a stethoscope on top of it.'

She wanted the blood-glucose monitor it contained. The glucose jell or IM glucagon or possibly even the IV glucose and the means of administering it.

'What's your name?' she asked again. 'Mine's Fiona.'

'Joe.' The word was a mumble and the lad's eyes were drifting shut.

'Have you got some jelly beans or anything with you, Joe?' It would be preferable to try and get some glucose on board orally but his level of consciousness was decreasing rapidly. Fiona felt the pockets of his jacket. Most diabetics carried some form of readily absorbed glucose like jelly beans or barley-sugar sweets.

Sure enough, she found a small packet of jelly beans.

'Ooh, black!' Fiona's smile felt a bit rusty. There hadn't been much to smile about for what seemed like a very long time. 'My favourite. Try and eat one of these for me, Joe.' She poked a jelly bean into his mouth. 'Chew it up,' she urged.

Agonisingly slowly, Joe complied. Fiona watched him, ready with a second jelly bean, as she waited for the police officer to return with her kit.

He was about the same age Nick had been when Fiona had met him for the first time.

'I've got a kid brother,' Al had warned her. *'He's geeky and gawky but he's OK.'*

Nick had been more than OK as far as Fiona was concerned. She might have been swept off her feet and totally in love with Alistair, the international rally car superstar, not to mention overawed by his equally famous parents, but Nick was the family member she had known she'd had the most in common with.

He was clever and focussed, not geeky.

Young and a bit shy, not gawky.

Fiona slipped another jelly bean into Joe's mouth. 'You're doing great,' she told him.

This time the chewing was just a little more enthusiastic. She even caught the hint of a smile as a corner of Joe's mouth lifted.

Nick's smile had been elusive to start with as well. Until the end of that weekend when Fiona had escaped the filming of a television interview. She'd gone for a walk despite the recent heavy snow. Without thinking, Fiona had taken the easy path left by someone's footprints and she'd caught up with Nick somewhere on the airfield. Somehow, they'd ended up making a snowman. Having a snowball fight. Even making snow angels by lying in the drifts and sweeping their arms up and down.

Nick's shyness had evaporated then. He'd smiled at the very idea of making a snowman and he'd laughed when his first snowball had been far more accurate than Fiona's and elicited a shriek as icy particles had gone down her neck. By the time they'd headed home they'd had flaming red cheeks, frozen fingers and toes and sides that ached from laughing. And, more, they had established a real connection. A genuine friendship.

Or so she'd believed at the time. Even then, Fiona had thought what a fabulous uncle Nick would make to her children. Children he'd probably known his brother never intended having.

What was he going to say when he learned about Sam? Or had he received that letter after all and had decided not to bother responding? Like he hadn't bothered to come to his only sibling's funeral.

'Is this what you wanted?'

'Yes…thanks…' Fiona shoved the old hurt aside yet again and dragged her thoughts back to the task at hand, but Joe was already responding to his oral glucose intake. He blinked at Fiona.

'I've had a hypo, haven't I?'

'Yeah…I'm just going to check your glucose level. Have another jelly bean while I prick your finger.'

'I missed lunch. I knew I was getting low so I went to get something to eat.' Joe's words were slow and a bit muffled by jelly beans. 'I had a hot dog in my hand when that car spun out. I dropped it and then…' He sent a dazed glance behind Fiona. 'I don't really remember. Was anyone killed?'

'No. There's a few people with serious injuries but they're all on their way to hospital.' Fiona was waiting for the test strip to be analysed by the small monitor. 'How are *you* feeling now?'

'A bit rubbish.'

'You'll need more than jelly beans. Maybe you'd better come down to the hospital for a while until you come right. Do you often have trouble managing your diabetes?'

'No. I'm usually good. This was my own fault.'

The monitor beeped and Fiona looked at the screen. 'Still on the low side. You need some more glucose and then something longer-acting, like some carbs.'

'I'll be OK. My girlfriend's here somewhere. She'll be wondering where I am. Oh…God!' Joe blinked again, focussing more intently on their surroundings. 'Was she hurt? Her name's Melanie. She's got long red hair and…and she's really pretty.'

Fiona touched his arm reassuringly. 'She wasn't one of the more seriously injured, anyway. Look, we'll get this police officer to make some enquiries. You come with me into the tent. That way I can keep an eye on you and we'll know where to find you when we locate Melanie.'

Joe was perfectly co-operative now, although somewhat wobbly as he climbed to his feet. His lanky frame uncurled to a height of well over six feet and Fiona could feel all his ribs as she put an arm around the young man to steady him.

He still had some growing to do. Maybe he would fill out to the kind of solid, muscular frame that Nick had finally developed in the six years since Fiona had last seen him. It was surprising just how imposing a figure her brother-in-law had become. Shocking, actually.

And not just physically. Nick had an aura of confidence. Of being in command. The kind of charisma Al had had. Or was it? This was confusing, the way the differences between the brothers had somehow blurred. Was it because Nick must now be thirty—much closer to the age that Al had been when he'd died and the only way Fiona could remember him?

Or was it because Nick had been involved in possibly countless situations that had called for the demonstration of advanced skills under extreme pressure? The kind of ability that automatically bestowed that kind of confidence. Nick's abilities might be used to save someone's life rather than entertain a huge crowd, but was the background intelligence and courage needed all that dissimilar?

He was a Stewart after all, and charisma had seemed genetic in that family.

Her son had those genes as well.

Fiona suddenly had the overwhelming urge to hear the sound of her little boy's voice. To reassure herself that he was safe. She would check the remaining patients in the triage tent and then take a minute or two to call her mother's cellphone.

'Sit down here,' she instructed Joe. 'We'll do another blood-glucose level in a few minutes.'

But Joe stayed standing. He was staring over Fiona's

shoulder to where the police officer was entering the tent
behind them, with a young woman by his side.

'Joe!'

'Mel!'

'I couldn't find you.' The young woman with long
auburn hair threw herself into Joe's outstretched arms. 'I
was so worried…'

'What's happened? Why have you got a bandage on
your arm?'

'I fell over. It's probably just a sprain. People were
pushing and running to get away. I was trying to go the
other way to get to the hot-dog stand.' Mel was crying now.
'The car crashed into it and I knew you were in the queue
and…'

'It's OK,' Joe said. 'I'm fine…'

'It *is* OK,' Fiona confirmed. 'Let's get both of you into
the bus and down to the hospital.'

'I can do that,' the police officer said. He was smiling
at this joyous reunion in front of them. A moment of relief
and happiness in the wake of such a terrible ordeal.

'Excuse me.' An exhausted-looking race official
touched Fiona's arm. 'We've got someone that can trans-
late now. Could you come and check the drivers?'

Fiona nodded. As she turned, she noticed an altercation
going on at the doorway of the tent as people holding television cameras and fluffy microphones on poles were
being refused entry.

She couldn't stop to ring her mother just yet and Fiona
could only hope they had gone home long ago. And that
nobody knew of Nick's connections.

Imagine the level of interest if the media caught the
angle that Al Stewart's brother—now an emergency physician—had found himself having to work in a situation

that must have been a dreadful reminder of the way his brother had died.

And then they'd find out about Sam and their lives would never be the same.

Fiona unhooked her stethoscope from around her neck in preparation for the thorough assessment she intended to give the Hungarian men. She could feel an odd knot in her stomach that she knew had nothing to do with the level of injuries she might be about to assess.

It was more to do with a sudden conviction that something irrevocable had already happened.

In what seemed almost like a very personal Scandinavian flick, her life had just taken a very unexpected and alarmingly sharp turn.

CHAPTER THREE

'I GUESS it's one way of getting a feel for the place.'

'You could say that.' Nick smiled somewhat wearily at the man he'd been working alongside for the last three hours. Then he nodded at the bottle of tablets a nurse held out as she walked past.

'Thanks, Megan. Tell Jeff to take one three times a day until they're finished. He's to come back if he's feeling unwell or notices any changes to his hand, like sensation dropping or pain increasing. We'll want to reassess him in a couple of days as well, so he'll need an outpatient appointment. Oh, and could you find him a salbutamol inhaler, please? Seems he's lost his.'

Hugh Patterson eyed the bottle of tablets. 'Antibiotics? Which one was Jeff?'

'Local guy. Freelance journalist. Got his middle finger ripped off and index finger broken.'

'You don't want to admit him?'

'I tried to but he won't stay. Says he just wants to get home. He's pretty shocked. I couldn't come up with a good enough reason to keep him. The wound's sorted and the fracture's set. Nothing we can do about the missing finger and there's no evidence of neurological damage to the rest of his hand.'

'That's lucky.'

'He doesn't think so. Seems to think his career is over. I hope the girlfriend who's coming to get him is supportive. He needs a bit of TLC.'

'Speaking of which…' Hugh smiled '…it's high time we actually sat down for a cup of coffee. Come with me and I'll show you our staffroom. I don't know about you but I'm exhausted.'

'It's certainly been full on. Not unlike a triage station in some of the war zones I've been in.'

'And hardly what you expected to find here.' Hugh was leading the way to the staffroom. 'Thanks for your help, mate. Lucky for us you decided to arrive and check out the place before you started work. We'd never have coped without you today.'

Nick negated the statement with a shake of his head, barely registering the staff noticeboard they were passing. There were baby photographs that stood out, though, and an advertisement for a pair of skis someone wanted to sell. 'I've been more than impressed with your set-up here, Hugh. Who's that nurse manager of yours?'

'Lizzie,' Hugh said proudly. 'She's great, isn't she?'

'So's that radiographer you called in. Steve? He's done a brilliant job.'

'Still doing it, in fact. He's got one of our last patients in with him now. Girl with red hair and a possible wrist fracture.'

'Melanie. Yes, I saw her a while back.'

The staffroom bench was cluttered with mugs nobody had found time to wash yet. The central table was just as cluttered, with paperwork being sorted by Shane and Fiona, who gave Hugh an apologetic smile.

'Sorry, Hugh. We were going to take all this back to the station but we would have had trouble finding enough space for this lot. Plus, we keep having to find the patients or their relatives to try and get more of their details.'

'Hey, no problem.' Hugh opened a cupboard to search for clean mugs. 'You've had at least two months' worth of trauma in one afternoon. I'll have to face the nightmare of my own paperwork shortly and it'll be a hell of lot easier if I have yours to work from. Want coffee?'

'Sure. Thanks.' Fiona's gaze shifted. 'Thanks again for your help up on the hill, Nick. Not the afternoon's entertainment you expected, was it?'

'Not exactly, no.'

Something in his tone made Hugh pause in his task of spooning coffee into mugs and give Nick a curious glance.

'You've obviously met Fi, then,' he said. 'You been introduced to Shane as well?'

'Not properly.' Nick held his hand out to the young paramedic. 'I'm Nick,' he said as they shook hands. 'Nick Stewart.'

'*Stewart?*' Shane frowned. 'Why does that name ring a bell?'

'It was my married name,' Fiona reminded him.

'Oh, that's right.' Shane raised his eyebrows at Nick. 'So you're related to Fi?'

'Good grief, that never occurred to me.' The jar of sugar Hugh was holding remained unopened. '*Are* you?'

For a moment, Nick said nothing, caught once again by Fiona's gaze.

She wasn't a Stewart any more?

Had she remarried?

'Brother-in-law,' he said slowly. How much did these people know about Fi? How much did she want them to know? She wasn't looking perturbed. Nick even caught the ghost of an encouraging nod. 'At least, I used to be.'

'Wow!' Shane's head swivelled towards his colleague. 'Did you know Nick was coming to visit?'

He couldn't read her expression as Fiona shook her head. A mix of denial and disbelief certainly, but there was something else there as well.

'It was the last thing I expected,' she said.

And the last thing she wanted, perhaps?

'Didn't think so.' Shane nodded. 'Weird, huh? You mention Al's brother for the first time only this afternoon and then—poof!—he appears.' He grinned. 'Spooky!'

'Maybe I have psychic powers,' Fiona said lightly.

Again, Nick said nothing. She had been talking about him to his partner? She remembered him?

'Boy.' Shane was grinning at Nick. 'Sam's going to be thrilled to meet you.'

'Sam?' Nick's lips froze halfway into a smile. Any pleasure in being remembered went out the window. So she *had* remarried.

'Your nephew,' Hugh put in helpfully.

Nick stared at Fiona. There was no mistaking the unease in those widened eyes.

'But I haven't—'

'Met him?' Shane's interruption was intended to be as helpful as Hugh had been. 'Yeah, I know. Fi said. You'll love him. Cutest four-year-old I've ever known.'

Hugh was ferrying mugs of coffee to the table. 'Only because my wee guy isn't that old yet.'

Fiona's grin looked a little forced. 'You're as bad as Maggie, Hugh. It's not a competition for who's got the cutest son. Luke and Sam are equally gorgeous.'

Nick was the only person not smiling.

Fi had a son? It couldn't be Al's child and therefore it couldn't be his own nephew. If she'd been pregnant at the

time of Al's death, the media would have had a field day
with the news and he would have known about it because
he'd read or seen every moment of the coverage.

He stared at Fiona. She was a mother? Who was the
father of her son? Nick wanted to escape. To find some
time alone. He had wanted to get his head around simply
seeing Fi again but that task had just become one hell of
a lot more complicated.

Fi was staring back and, oddly, there was accusation
in her gaze.

Anger, even.

Nick gave his head an imperceptible shake. He was
missing something here.

Something huge.

Hugh seemed unaware of any undercurrents but, then,
his attention was on taking his first sip of coffee. With an
appreciative sigh he leaned back against the bench and
then gave Nick a thoughtful glance.

'So—did you get my email the other day? About the
house?'

'No, sorry. I've been on the move. I was going to catch
up with mail at my hotel tonight.' Nick swallowed some
of his own coffee . He couldn't help his gaze sliding back
towards Fiona but she had her head bent, a hand on her
forehead, shielding her eyes, and she was writing something on a case report form. The impression that she was
deliberately avoiding involvement in this conversation was
unmistakable but Nick wasn't offended.

He knew exactly how she was feeling.

Fiona needed space to get her head around things as
much as he did.

'You don't need a hotel,' Hugh said dismissively.
'There's doctors' quarters right here at the hospital.'

'The hotel's fine.' Nick wasn't going on the payroll until next week and he wouldn't be happy accepting staff privileges before then. 'I was planning to be a tourist for a few days. I've never been to Queenstown. Never even been to New Zealand before.'

Fiona was scribbling rapidly, apparently absorbed by writing a patient history, but Shane's paperwork had been forgotten.

'You'll love it,' he told Nick. 'You're probably into adventure sports. You can go skiing, white-water rafting, bungee-jumping—'

'Whoa!' Nick shook his head. 'I came here for the clean, green space, not an adrenaline rush.'

Shane looked disappointed but then he rallied. 'I guess you've had your fair share of excitement. Fi said you were with…what was it?'

'Médecins Sans Frontières,' Fiona supplied quietly, without looking up.

So she wasn't that absorbed with her paperwork after all. Nick knew he probably had a puzzled frown on his face as he stared at the top of her head. Maybe she sensed his attention because she glanced up briefly. And there it was again. The accusation. Did she have something against MSF? Was that the problem?

'What's that when it's at home?' Shane queried.

'It means doctors without borders,' Nick explained. 'It's an international humanitarian aid organisation. It's purpose is to provide emergency medical assistance to people in danger.'

'You've done that for a while, haven't you?' Hugh said.

'Nearly six years.' Nick closed his eyes for a second. 'Long enough.'

'Yeah.' Hugh's tone was sympathetic. 'It must be draining.'

'Where did you go?' Shane asked.

'Lots of places. Indonesia, Malaysia, Iraq, Ecuador…' Nick's voice trailed off. It wasn't what he wanted to talk about right now.

'And you come for some time out to peaceful, rural New Zealand,' Hugh said gently, 'and look what we throw at you. My apologies.'

Nick found a smile. 'I'm not holding you responsible, Hugh.'

'I'd like to make up for it anyway. Look, if you don't fancy the doctors' quarters, come home with me. The place is a bombsite, what with packing for the trip, but Maggie would love to meet you. In fact, I'll be in trouble if I don't take you home.'

'I…ah…' Nick didn't want to be whisked off to the hospitality of the Patterson household, however warm that was likely to be. What he wanted was a chance to talk to Fiona.

'That way, you can check the place out and see if you think Maggie's idea might work,' Hugh continued.

'Maggie's idea?' Nick was only half listening.

Why wasn't Fiona saying anything? Was she just trying to find some space for a few moments or was she going to avoid spending time with him for the whole of his month-long stay? If so, what was supposed to be the start of a new direction could turn out to be a total disaster.

'That you house-sit for us. Look after the dogs and—'

Fiona abruptly stopped her scribbling. She stared at Hugh. 'I thought you were going to get your locum to do that.'

There was a moment's silence and the penny finally dropped. Fiona looked from Nick to Hugh and back again.

'*You're* the locum?'

'Yes.'

Another tiny silence. This time the undercurrents were obvious to everyone but Fiona couldn't summon even a polite smile that could indicate that this was a pleasant surprise. It was stunning. Not only had Nick reappeared in her life like a bolt of lightning from a clear sky, he was there to stay.

At least, that's how it felt right now. A whole month seemed like for ever.

Hugh cleared his throat. An uncomfortable sound that advertised the realisation of issues that could potentially undermine the carefully laid plans to cover his absence.

'I'd better get back out to the front line.' Hugh put his empty mug into the sink. 'Steve should have finished those X-rays by now.'

'And I'd better start filing this paperwork,' Fiona said hurriedly. 'Before it buries us.'

'I can do that.' Shane responded to a meaningful glance from Hugh as the consultant left the staffroom. He started gathering the forms.

'Leave the top copies for Hugh,' Fiona instructed. 'And put the rest on my desk. I might check them over again before I head home in case I've missed something.'

She could have taken the forms away herself but the look Hugh had given Shane hadn't gone unnoticed. He was trying to leave her alone with Nick and there had been an unspoken plea that a major issue could be avoided in the run-up to him leaving the country for an extended period.

A plea that was being echoed in the expression on Nick's face as the others left the room.

'Is it a problem for you, Fi?' he asked quietly. 'Me being the locum here?'

'No!' The word was emphatic. Hugh and Maggie were Fiona's best friends. She owed it to them to make sure this wasn't going to be a problem. 'I'm...I'm just surprised, that's all. This is the last place I would have expected to see you.'

'Likewise.'

Fiona's breath escaped in an incredulous huff. 'But you knew this was where I grew up. That my parents lived here.'

'Did I?' Nick looked genuinely perplexed as he moved to sit at the end of the table, just an arm's length from Fiona. 'I knew you came from New Zealand but I don't think I ever made a connection to a particular place, and even if I did, I had no idea you'd come back. When *did* you come back?'

'The day after Al's funeral.' Fiona was watching Nick carefully. Would she see any regret? An apology for not being there?

Strangely, she got the fleeting impression of something more like relief.

'What time did you leave?'

'What?'

'What time of day was it?'

'I don't remember.' This was ridiculous. They had such a lot they could, *should*, be talking about and he wanted to know what time of day she had caught a plane? 'Why on earth does it matter?' she heard herself snapping. 'You weren't even there.'

The old resentment bubbled up and now that the adrenaline rush of dealing with a major incident had gone, leaving exhaustion in its wake, it was too much. To her horror, Fiona felt the prickle of tears.

'*Why* weren't you there, Nick?' Her voice caught. 'I know you and Al had fallen out but couldn't you at least have come to his funeral?'

'I did.'

Fiona swallowed painfully. *'What?'*

'I was there, Fi. I almost didn't make it. It was incredibly difficult to get connecting flights out of Ecuador. I arrived late at Heathrow and by the time I got through the traffic and arrived at the service, I was stuck behind the media contingent. I couldn't get anywhere near you.'

'You can't have tried very hard.'

'That's not fair.' There was an edge of anger in his voice that startled Fiona. Nick had never been the angry one—that had been Al's domain. Had he become like his brother in more ways than simply an increase in physical build?

Hopefully not, but Fiona found she was holding her breath as she waited for his next words. Bracing herself automatically for some kind of personal attack.

It didn't happen. Nick's words carried an undertone of defeat. He sounded as weary as she was feeling.

'Did you have any idea how protective those people around you were?'

Fiona shook her head slowly. 'Not really.'

In retrospect, those days had become a blur. The worst days of her life. She could remember begging for privacy, though. Asking everyone she could to help shield her from the media. And to shield those closest to her although her mother had been the only family member to be by her side.

'Why didn't you just tell them who you were?'

'And have the spotlight turned on me? Don't you remember how much I hated it? I told you, didn't I? I was always the invisible kid.' A seemingly pent-up bitterness grew in intensity as he spoke and there was a hard edge that, again, Fiona would never have expected from Nick. He *had* grown up, hadn't he?

'The only way anybody ever noticed me was as Alistair's brother. The shadow.' The anger was muted now but the aftermath of bitterness spoke volumes. 'I didn't want to be the shadow at the last photo shoot he was ever going to have. To get attention because I was the only surviving Stewart. To see what everybody would have been thinking…that the wrong brother had died.'

'*Nick!*' Quite unconsciously, along with the horrified intake of her breath, Fiona had reached out and had taken hold of his hand. 'It wasn't like that.'

But it had been, hadn't it? It was how they'd connected in the first place. They had both been like fish out of water in a family that had craved public adulation. Maybe Nick had only ever revealed the tip of the iceberg.

Had he really felt so unwanted as a child? Had that had something to do with why the brothers had stopped talking to each other? How had Fiona missed how big an issue it had been? She'd been guilty of thinking the same things herself, hadn't she? That Nick was the shadow. Quiet. Thoughtful. Gentle. All the attributes that Al had missed out on, really.

All this time Fiona had felt resentful that Nick hadn't been at the funeral to support her.

But it had been Nick that had needed that support even more than she had. She hadn't tried to find him, had she? She'd been upset he hadn't come. Had convinced herself that she meant nothing to him. That their friendship had never been genuine. As false as the vows Al had made on their wedding day had turned out to be.

'Nick, I'm sorry.' Fiona squeezed his hand. 'I wish I'd seen you but I was just trying to get through the ordeal and escape the cameras. I barely looked at anyone.'

Nick's smile was crooked. 'You wouldn't have recognised me even if you had spotted me. I'd grown a beard. Easier than trying to shave every day in places like Ecuador.'

The bitterness had gone from his tone but Fiona still wanted to make amends. To ease the awful guilt that was taking over that stupid resentment she'd harboured all these years.

'Why did you ask about the time of day I left London?'

'Because I tried to ring you. I rang and rang the following afternoon and got no answer.'

'I left at about lunchtime. Mum had to get back because Dad was in hospital. Here, in fact. He'd had another stroke. It was her idea that I came back with her and somebody pulled some strings and got me a ticket. I didn't know you were in London, Nick. Nobody told me.'

'I didn't tell anybody. I wanted to keep it quiet.'

'I didn't have anything to stay for and I was worried about Dad.'

'Of course you were. It never occurred to me that you might have gone away, though. When I finally had my call answered, a woman told me that you didn't want to talk to anyone. Even when I told her who I was, she said you weren't taking calls. From anyone.'

'I had someone stay in the house to make it look like I was still there. I didn't want to be followed. I thought if I bought enough time, the story would be of no interest to anyone. And then, when I found out I was pregnant, it was really important that no one knew where I was.'

'I wrote letters but they just got sent back.'

'I changed back to my maiden name. There's only a few people here that know the connection and they love Sam. They want to protect him as much as Mum and I do.'

Fiona was still holding Nick's hand. She could feel a

tear escaping but she was smiling at the same time. She could make amends. She could not only get rid of a shadow from her past that had haunted her, she could make life better for the people she loved the most.

'You'll love him, Nick. He looks…' Fiona's gaze was slightly blurred but she could see the features of the man sitting so close to her clearly enough. A blunted version of the rugged good looks Al had had. Softer but with the same floppy, dark hair, the same brown eyes, the wide smile that came more slowly with Nick but could still light up a room.

'He looks a lot like you,' she finished softly.

'So he really is my nephew?'

Fiona let the implied insult pass. Of course this was a shock. Sam was now the only close blood relative Nick Stewart had in the world.

'I was nearly five months pregnant by the time I found out. I thought the stress of Al's death and then coming home and helping to look after Dad had been responsible for making my cycles irregular. I was so…I guess shocked is the only word for it, really.'

'Yeah…' Nick's gaze had softened. 'I know the feeling.'

'It feels weird, doesn't it?' As Fiona held his gaze she realised she was *still* holding Nick's hand and it suddenly felt completely inappropriate. She let it go and her smile felt embarrassed.

Curiously shy, even.

'It *is* good to see you, Nick. I've often thought how much Sam would love to meet his uncle.'

Nick had pulled his abandoned hand closer to his body. He looked away and cleared his throat. Was he embarrassed as well? Then he nodded. Slowly, giving the impression that something was falling into place in his head. When he looked back at Fiona his gaze was steady and the slow smile so like the Nick she remembered that an odd, melting sensation happened somewhere inside her chest.

The kind of sensation she now associated with moments when she checked on Sam late at night and stood looking down at her sleeping son.

'I can't wait to meet him,' Nick said.

'Come home with me,' Fiona urged. 'The house isn't huge but we'll find room.'

'I don't need to stay. I've got a hotel I can go to.'

'No.' Fiona shook her head firmly. 'You can't go to a hotel, Nick. No way.'

'Why not?'

'Because…I want you to meet Sam. And my mum.'

She could see the uncertainty in his face but she could also see longing, and Fiona's heart squeezed again as she wondered if this man had always felt left out. She had a glimpse of the boy she remembered and a sudden insight that he could have been running all these years because he hadn't had somewhere he could feel like he belonged. Somewhere he was genuinely loved and wanted.

He had been Al's kid brother.

He was her son's uncle.

And quite apart from those connections, he was, simply, Nick.

'Come home,' she said softly. 'You're *family*, Nick. It's where you belong.'

CHAPTER FOUR

'BUT I've got *lots* of uncles.' The small boy in Fiona's arms had a singularly unimpressed expression as he took another look over his shoulder at the newcomer his mother had brought home. 'There's Uncle Hugh and Uncle Steve and Uncle Shane and—'

'Good heavens!' Fiona's mother, Elsie Murchison, gave an embarrassed laugh. 'It sounds like you have endless men in tow, Fi.'

'They're friends,' Fiona said casually. 'And all good role models.' She gave her son another cuddle and then set him down onto a well-worn carpet that suited the old house. 'Nick's different, sweetheart. He's your *real* uncle. He was your daddy's brother.'

'Oh, my!' Elsie said, not for the first time. She wiped her hands on her apron. 'I still can't believe it. It's been... How long has it been, Fi? Since the wedding?'

'Ten years.'

Nick didn't want the inevitable awkward pause to emphasise the breakdown of the bond he had once had with these people. 'You don't look a day older, Mrs Murchison.'

'Call me Elsie,' Fiona's mother instructed. Then she flapped her hand and smiled broadly. 'And flattery will get

you everywhere, young man. Come in! Don't stay
standing by the door. You're family after all.' She beamed
at Nick. 'This is…*wonderful*!'

Sam's eyes were the size of saucers. He watched Nick
walk further into the lounge and find a seat on one of the
sofas near a log fire that was burning merrily.

'Were you friends with my daddy?'

Nick dragged his gaze from the cluster of framed photographs on the mantelpiece. Baby photographs of Sam.
Pictures of Fiona with her parents. A large photograph of
Alistair in his racing colours, holding an enormous silver
trophy aloft and with a grin that couldn't advertise anything other than triumph.

'Sometimes.' Nick smiled at Sam but the humour went
over the child's head. 'He was my big brother,' he added,
with another, involuntary glance at the photograph. 'He
was really important and clever and brave.'

'He raced *cars*!'

Nick nodded gravely. 'I know.'

'Like the ones I saw today with Ga.'

'Ga?'

Fiona came to his rescue. 'Sam had trouble with
"Grandma" when he started talking and "Ga" kind of
stuck.' She turned her to mother and lowered her voice.
'How much did he see?'

Elsie gave her head a small, reassuring shake. 'We heard
the crash, of course, and saw smoke but that was all. We were
talking to Bernie Johns, of all people. I went to school with
Bernie and hadn't seen him for more than forty years…
Anyway,' Elsie dismissed the conversational distraction. 'We
came straight home. I've heard a bit on the news since…'

Her expression was questioning but Fiona echoed the
headshake. Not in front of Sam, the gesture said. Her arm

moved as well, a protective touch that brushed the top of the dark head close to her leg.

'Do you race cars, too?' Sam asked Nick.

'No.' Nick kept his smile with difficulty. Was Alistair's son going to make him feel like he didn't make the grade? Could it be an inherited talent?

'Do you know…' Fiona bent her head and spoke with the air of someone imparting a secret '…that your uncle Nick is a doctor—just like Uncle Hugh.'

Sam's gaze was assessing. His nod suggested that being a doctor was an acceptable profession. 'Luke's my friend,' he announced. 'We play cars. Would you like to see my cars?'

'Sure.'

Fiona had turned to her mother. 'Nick's here as a locum for Hugh,' she said. 'He's going to be here for a month.'

'Oh, my! Did you know he was coming? Why didn't you say something?'

'I didn't know. I'm sure Hugh never mentioned a name. He just said it was someone who came with astonishingly good references in the field of emergency medicine.'

Nick shrugged modestly but Fiona smiled. 'You more than lived up to your reputation today and you haven't even officially started work.'

Again, the reminder of what had happened at the rally created a blip in the conversation and the adults all glanced at the child in their midst, who was making his way towards the sofa, a toy car clutched in each hand. Nick could see that Sam was aware of the attention. He even gave the impression that he was aware of the undercurrents, though he might not understand them.

'There was a crash today,' he said to Nick in a stage whisper as he climbed onto the sofa beside him.

'I know,' Nick whispered back. 'I was there, too.'

'My mummy had to help fix the people who got hurt.'

'Nick was helping, too,' Fiona said.

'Did the driver get hurt, Mummy?'

'Not badly, sweetheart.'

Sam turned back to Nick. 'My daddy got hurt in a crash,' he said matter-of-factly. 'That's why he's not here any more. He's deaded.'

Nick glanced at Fiona with concern but she seemed perfectly at ease with the exchange. Did they talk about Al a lot? Enough to make him more of a presence in this household than just an image on the mantelpiece?

It felt that way.

And it felt odd.

A link to a past Nick had left behind such a long time ago.

A link he had chosen to break himself, well before the death of their parents had removed the anchor of a shared family home. He couldn't help a sweeping glance around the comfortable room he was in right now. There were lots of books and photographs. Toys strewn around the floor. Washing that was waiting to be folded using up an armchair. The smell of something delicious wafting in from the kitchen.

His childhood home had never felt like this. How could it have when his parents had used their dwelling as an advertisement for their wealth and status? When they'd died it had become apparent they had lived beyond their means so there hadn't been too much of an inheritance for their sons but, as Al's widow, Fi must have inherited millions. It had to be a deliberate choice to live modestly. Part of protecting Sam, maybe?

If so, the little boy was lucky. Life might have been

very different if Nick had grown up in a home like this. One that was clearly filled with love and laughter and good things to eat.

Elsie seemed to be reading his thoughts. 'Dinner's almost ready,' she said. 'Sam, could you move your paper and crayons off the table, please?'

'But I'm showing Uncle Nick my cars. See?' A small red and white toy was shoved close to Nick's face.

'Later,' Fiona said. 'There'll be plenty of time before you go to bed and Uncle Nick might even stay with us for a few days.'

'But—'

'You could use Sam's room,' Fiona continued. 'Sam still sneaks into my bed as often as not, anyway.' She wasn't going to allow time for any protest from Nick. 'Excuse me for a few minutes,' she said. 'I'm going to jump into the shower so I can get out of this uniform. Can I get you a glass of wine or something?'

'I'll do that,' Elsie said. 'And I'll talk Nick into staying while you get changed. Red or white wine, Nick? Sorry, but we don't have a beer at the moment.'

'A glass of red would be fantastic,' Nick said. 'Thank you.'

Elsie held out her hand to her grandson as Fiona left the room. 'Sam, do you think you could find a packet of crisps in the cupboard?'

'For me?' Sam slid off the couch with a grin that gave Nick a jolt. It was so like Al's grin. Radiating the kind of charm that had always won him instant friends.

'For you *and* Uncle Nick. You can share.'

Sam trotted after Elsie towards the source of the wonderful smell. 'I'm good at sharing, aren't I, Ga?'

'You are, darling. Very good.'

Nick found himself sitting alone on a sofa. Or not quite alone. A small red and white car was on the cushion beside him. He picked it up without thinking, staring at the object without really seeing it.

This feeling of total bemusement was foreign. It probably had a lot to do with displacement. Jet-lag. The aftermath of dealing with some horrific trauma that had shattered lives as well as limbs today.

But a large part of it stemmed from seeing Fiona again. It was like someone had taken his life and shaken it. The places he had been, the people he had known, the things he had learned seemed fragmented. Any sense of moving forward or even continuity had been disrupted to a point that was leaving him confused.

Almost lost.

Nick leaned back with a sigh and closed his eyes for a moment. The feeling was not pleasant and that in itself was confusing because this room—the whole atmosphere of this small house and the warmth of the people it contained—had to be one of the most pleasant places he had ever been.

An ability to rinse away both the grime and the emotional involvement in her work was a skill Fiona had developed as a mother. As much as was possible, Sam became her focus as soon as she stepped over the threshold of her home.

Usually, by the time her uniform was discarded in favour of her favourite faded denim jeans and the soft, clinging merino wool tops she loved, Fiona would be well on the way to shutting down the professional compartment of her brain. Or, at least, putting it on standby.

Something felt different tonight, however. Standing in

the still steamy bathroom, Fiona brushed out the kinks her braid had left in her hair and found she was still thinking about medical matters.

Not so strange, really, given the magnitude of the incident they'd had to deal with today. Any one of those cases were the sort that Fiona would want to discuss at length with Hugh when they both had the time and energy. To go over her assessment and treatment and see if there was anything she could have done better.

She could do that with Nick while it was all still fresh in her mind. Gain a new perspective on pre-hospital emergency care from someone more qualified than herself who was very experienced in working on the front line, from all accounts so far. The attraction of that possibility was unsettling in itself because Fiona had worked hard to separate home and work compartments and create the haven her son deserved.

By the time Fiona returned to the lounge she had dismissed the notion of such a discussion. There were too many other things she wanted to talk to Nick about when Sam had gone to bed.

Personal things.

A burning curiosity was beginning to surface. Why was Nick here? Why was he still single? Or did he have a partner—a *wife*, even—who was planning to join him in New Zealand?

And why was that idea as unsettling as anything else to do with this man's sudden reappearance in her life?

The man responsible for her mental disruption was currently lying on his stomach on the floor of the lounge, bathed in the glow of firelight, head to head with a small boy in an identical pose. They both had small cars in their hands and they were driving them around a bowl that contained what looked like crisp crumbs. They were also both making enthusiastic engine noises.

Fiona started to smile but something caught her lips and made them wobble.

Would Al—the superstar rally driver—have ever lain on an old carpet and played with his son like this?

A ghostly laugh played somewhere in the back of her mind.

'Kids? Me? Not in this lifetime, babe.'

The carpet really was getting too old. The wheels of Sam's bright blue car caught on a patch of exposed threads.

'I'm stuck, Uncle Nick!' He yanked the toy and a small metal bar with a plastic wheel on each end popped off. 'Oh, no!' Sam cried forlornly. 'I'm *broken*!'

'Pit stop,' Nick said calmly. He took the pieces of the toy and clicked the wheels back into place. The movement brought Fiona into his line of vision.

Nick grinned, seemingly unembarrassed at his rather undignified position, and then Sam grinned up at his mother and the likeness between the adult and child was unmistakable.

Stupidly, Fiona actually had to blink back tears. *This* was what was missing in Sam's life, wasn't it? It didn't matter how many wonderful male role models she had available, there was something about a family tie that just couldn't be replicated.

Elsie saved her from anyone noticing her reaction.

'Dinner's ready,' she announced, wiping her hands on her apron as she came into the lounge. 'Sam, why don't you go and get your pyjamas on?'

'But I want dinner, too, Ga.'

'You had your dinner, darling. Before Mummy came home, remember? You must be getting tired by now.'

'No. I'm not tired.' Sam held his eyelids open as widely as possible with his fingers. 'See?'

Everybody laughed as Nick and Sam got to their feet but then Sam started coughing. A dry cough that became more noticeable as they all sat down at the table, where Elsie's roast chicken sat on a big platter surrounded by crisp vegetable portions.

He coughed again as Fiona poured some gravy over the tiny amount of chicken and potato she had placed on his plate.

'I think we'd better get your huffer, sweetheart.'

'I'll get it, Mummy.' Sam glanced at Nick to make sure he was listening and then added proudly, 'I know what to do.'

Nick paused before selecting a wedge of pumpkin to add to his plate. He watched Sam race towards the door. 'Asthma?' he queried.

'Just mild.' Fiona nodded. 'Responds well to medication.' She pushed her chair back. 'Excuse me for a second. I'll go and help him.'

'I had asthma when I was Sam's age.'

'*Did you?*' Fiona swung back to give Nick an astonished glance. 'I never knew that.'

Nick's shrug was almost a put down. Why should she have known? Had she ever been particularly interested in anyone other than his brother? The *important* Stewart son?

His smile told Fiona she was overreacting. 'It wasn't that big a deal,' he said. 'It might have contributed to my aversion to the kind of strenuous physical pursuits Al was so good at and it was kind of embarrassing that petrol fumes could set it off, but I grew out it eventually.'

'Let's hope Sam does, too.' Elsie nudged the platter. 'Help yourself to some more vegetables, Nick. There's plenty.'

The medication settled Sam's cough but all the excitement of the day caught up with him and, despite his best efforts, he was falling asleep well before it was time for the steamed treacle pudding Elsie had made for dessert.

'Time for bed,' Fiona said firmly.

Sam didn't protest. He was almost too tired to lift up his arms as Fiona picked him up from the chair. He rubbed his nose on her neck. 'Your bed,' he mumbled. ''Member, Mummy?'

'I remember.' Fiona shifted his weight. Just when had her baby become this heavy? 'You going to say goodnight to Ga, button?'

''Night, Ga.'

'And goodnight to Uncle Nick?'

Heavy eyelids fluttered. 'Can Uncle Nick tell me a story?'

'I think you're too tired for a story tonight, button. You'll be asleep by the time your head hits the pillow.'

'No-o-o...want a story, Mummy. The one 'bout Daddy.'

Fiona caught Nick's expression. 'It's one about a long race,' she explained. 'I don't think Sam's ever stayed awake to reach the finish flags.'

'I will.' Sam was rallying. 'If Uncle Nick tells me the story, I'll stay awake.'

'Uncle Nick doesn't know our story.' Fiona shifted the weight she was holding again and stifled a sigh. Getting Sam to bed was shaping up to be a longer process than normal.

'But...he was Daddy's brother...'

Embarrassingly, the small silence was loaded with something like obligation. Fiona gave Nick an apologetic glance. She hadn't dragged him home in order for him to perform a role as a family member. Not consciously, anyway. Or so immediately.

Nick's expression was unreadable as cleared his throat. 'I know a few stories about Al's races,' he said cautiously. 'I'm sure I could manage.'

'Go on, then.' Elsie seemed to think it was all perfectly acceptable. She stood up and started clearing the table. 'I'll have dessert ready by the time you get back.'

It felt really weird to have a large male figure following her along the villa's wide central hallway. Even more disconcerting to lead him into her own bedroom, which was lit only by the small lamp on her bedside table. Fiona took a deep breath and tried to make a joke of it.

'Congratulations.' She smiled. 'You're the first adult male to step into my room since...'

Since his brother had died.

Oh, *help*! Why on earth had she said that?

'In a long time,' she finished lamely. The blush came from nowhere and her cheeks were flaming as she used one hand to shift embroidered pillows and turn back a patchwork quilt.

'It's a lovely room.'

Maybe Nick hadn't noticed her gaffe. He was looking around him with apparent interest. At the seat set into the wide bay window with its lovely stained-glass fanlights. At the huge, free-standing kauri wardrobe, the cluttered bookcase and the faded family portrait on the wall beside the dressing-table.

'Is that you?'

Fiona glanced up again as she helped Sam snuggle beneath the duvet. The photograph had a small girl with two long braids sitting on a swing—a proud parent on either side. She grinned.

'Of course. Haven't changed that much, have I?'

'Your hair's long again. It was short the last time I saw you.'

'I'm just lazy. I should cut it off again. Kind of gets in the way for work sometimes.'

'No, don't do that! I like it.'

He was staring at her. The dim light should have made it less personal to hold the eye contact. Maybe it went on a fraction too long or maybe it was the way the corners of Nick's mouth lifted into what seemed like a very appreciative smile.

Whatever. It did something funny to Fiona's insides and she found she was blushing again. Hurriedly, she stooped and kissed Sam.

'Sound asleep,' she pronounced. 'No story needed, you'll be pleased to hear.'

With another soft touch to her son's head Fiona led the way from her room with more than a little relief. No doubt Nick was feeling the same way.

Or maybe not.

'I wouldn't have minded,' he said when they were in the hallway again.

'You sure?' Fiona caught his gaze deliberately. Searching his face. 'This can't be that easy for you, Nick. All these reminders of Al must be the last thing you expected.'

'It's worth it,' Nick said softly. 'I feel like I've found something I thought I'd lost for ever. Maybe even something I never *really* had. A…a family.'

He said the word as though it was something magical. Something too good to be true. And Fiona had the haunting impression that beneath the mature, confident exterior a lost and lonely man could be hiding.

That odd prickle inside her grew stronger.

It was easy to channel it and tap into her curiosity. Again, it felt personal enough to need a light approach.

'So you haven't got an adoring wife and six kids?'

'No.'

There it was again. That haunting note that touched something very deep. Too deep.

'How on earth has someone as gorgeous as you escaped for so long, Nick?'

He stopped moving. He was staring again and he looked…horrified?

Fiona gave herself a mental slap. She'd put her foot in her mouth again, hadn't she? Not that he *wasn't* gorgeous but—good grief! After her crack about having a man in her bedroom she might be giving her ex-brother-in-law the impression that she was coming on to him or something.

There was only one way out. Fiona laughed. Merrily, she hoped.

'I'm allowed to say things like that. I'm old and wise, remember? Old enough to be your mother, in fact.'

'Hardly.'

Yes. That was pushing credibility given there was only six years between them. It *had* seemed like a generation when they'd first met. Funny how the gap had shrunk so remarkably but that was probably only from her perspective. From Nick's viewpoint she was still a much older woman. Someone safe because she was practically family. No wonder he had looked so horrified. Reassurance was needed.

'Big sister, then,' she said firmly. 'Just like I always was.'

Nick said nothing and he didn't return her smile. More reassurance was clearly needed. Fiona gave him a sisterly sort of pat on the arm.

'Come on. Mum's treacle pudding is to die for. You'll love it.'

* * *

The pudding was hot, sticky and looked delicious, and Nick thought it tasted like sawdust.

It had been a terrible mistake to come here.

Not just to this house. He should have stayed on the other side of the globe.

He watched Fiona adding whipped cream and custard to her dessert. How did she stay so slim? Nick hadn't been able to help noticing how that soft red jersey she was wearing accentuated how flat her stomach was beneath the swell of her breasts. Or how those old jeans hugged smooth hips and the long legs he'd never forgotten.

Of course he had noticed.

Even with the gap of so many years and his best efforts to relegate his feelings to no more than a teenage crush, nothing had changed.

He was only half listening to the conversation Fiona was having with her mother.

'So he decided to come back to Queenstown. His wife died about the same time your dad did and his kids are scattered all over the world now.'

'And you went to school together?'

'The primary school only had two or three teachers in those days. Bernie was a couple of years older than me but we were always in the same class. We did a science project together once. It involved making an electric current by winding a handle.' Elsie was laughing. 'My job was to hold the other end and test whether it was working. I hated it!'

Fiona laughed as well. A soft sound that struck the same kind of chords in Nick's memory as the way her clothes fitted had done.

Were still doing. With a huge effort, Nick tried to join the conversation.

'So did this Bernie end up being an electrician?'

'No. He went into the police force, apparently. Ended up being a detective and solving all sorts of murders. Says he wants a very quiet retirement.'

'Sounds like you had a lot to talk about,' Fiona said.

'Mmm.' Elsie sounded almost coy. 'He's asked me out for dinner next week. And I said yes.'

'Really?' Fiona's spoon halted in mid-air. 'Good for you!'

'It doesn't mean anything,' Elsie said hurriedly. 'We just have a lot in common from the old days.'

Nick and Fiona had quite a lot in common from the old days but would she view that as a good thing?

'I wasn't suggesting anything,' Fiona was saying calmly. 'I think it's great. It's been three years since Dad died, Mum. It would be wonderful if you found someone whose company you enjoyed.'

It had been longer than that since Al had died. Why hadn't Fiona found someone? Maybe she had. Just because she hadn't had a man in her own bedroom it didn't mean that she didn't have a relationship. Discretion could simply be part of protecting her son.

It meant nothing.

Just like the startling way she had told him he was gorgeous meant nothing.

It was just as well Fiona could have no idea what the effect of those words had been. Nick forced himself to swallow the last spoonfuls of his dessert, trying to fight off a return of that unpleasant, life-disrupting, *shaken* sensation he had experienced earlier.

And he was failing miserably.

'You're very quiet, Nick.' Fiona and her mother had finished both their desserts and their conversation.

'Just a bit tired. Sorry. I've done a lot of travelling in the last week or so.'

Elsie took his bowl. 'Have you had enough to eat?'

'Too much. Thank you, it was wonderful.'

Fiona stood up. 'I'll go and change the sheets on Sam's bed. That way, you can crash as soon as you need to.'

He had already crashed, though, hadn't he? All those carefully constructed defences. Ten years of convincing himself that he'd been too young to know what love really was. That he'd find the right person. That he would never again experience that dreadful longing for something he could never have.

It had just been a careless query about his marital status. A few words that had given Nick an insight that had been as crushing as being relegated—again—to the status of simply a 'kid brother'.

It wasn't that he'd tried to avoid the responsibilities of having a wife and children. Far from it. It was just that until that moment he'd never understood why it had been such a frustrating mission to try and find the *right* woman. He'd been deluding himself.

There was no one else on earth remotely like Fi.

Nick gathered the strength he knew he was going to need. He pushed himself to his feet.

'I really ought to go back to my hotel. All my gear is there.'

'But—'

Nick had to look away from the disappointment in Fiona's eyes. She might see too much. With his defences knocked so hard by the emotional shaking he was experiencing, she might even still see that raw, vulnerable boy he'd once been.

Had Al ever told her what he'd discovered on the eve of their wedding?

If so, there was no way he could stay here.

But there was no way he *couldn't* stay either. There was a small boy not far away that Nick already felt an astonishing connection with. More than just a physical resemblance. Maybe it was the fact that Sam suffered from mild asthma—as he had done himself. Or maybe it had something to do with the hero-worship of Alistair, the superstar. It was almost like seeing a version of himself. Or what he could have been, before he'd become invisible.

He wanted to get to know his nephew.

Fiona was reading his thoughts. 'Sam will be terribly disappointed if you're not here in the morning.'

'It's only walking distance,' Nick heard himself saying. 'I could come back first thing in the morning and…and we'll be seeing a lot of each other in the next few weeks. You'll all be sick of the sight of me by then.'

'No.' Fiona was shaking her head slowly. 'We won't.'

'Why don't you walk back to your hotel and collect what you need?' Elsie was about to take a stack of dirty plates to the bench. 'And then come back. We want you here, Nick. You're *family*.'

It was easy to smile at Elsie but Nick's gaze was drawn instantly back to Fiona and the smile faded. The mix of emotions he could see was like looking into a mirror.

There was desire for something there but confusion as well. Trepidation, perhaps. An acknowledgement of barriers and a past that needed closure. But, surprisingly, there was something else.

Hope?

Nick's smile widened again. Tentatively. It felt almost like an admission of defeat. He couldn't run, could he? This might be the biggest challenge he'd ever faced in his life but he wouldn't be able to live with himself if he didn't give it his best shot

'If you're sure,' he said quietly. 'I would really like to stay. Just for a day or two. Until I'm sorted. Looking after Hugh's house sounds like a good idea.'

Fiona was nodding. 'You'll love it,' she said. 'It's perfect.'

Was she referring to his accommodation plans or the fact that they would be spending so much time together?

Nick could only hope she wouldn't find out how right she was.

Or how wrong.

CHAPTER FIVE

LAKEVIEW HOSPITAL'S small emergency department was back to normal.

Only a couple of the cubicle beds were occupied and the treatment room Fiona and Shane were pushing the stretcher towards was empty apart from the staff members who had been alerted to their incoming patient via radio communication.

Just what she would have expected on a quiet Tuesday afternoon.

Having Nick Stewart among the waiting team had not been expected but Fiona knew Hugh had been planning to give him a guided tour of the hospital today. They'd been talking about it last night when she had taken Nick to dinner at the Pattersons'. She also knew it was something she would have to get used to. Lakeview's medical director was the doctor most likely to be available in a department where patient numbers were not sufficient to justify a full-time consultant.

'This is Ricky Bennett,' she announced, as they drew the stretcher to a halt beside the bed. 'Twenty-one years old. He's sustained superficial and partial thickness burns to his right leg and foot, with some splash burns to his arms.'

A look passed between the two doctors.

'Go for it,' Hugh invited. 'This is going to be your department soon enough.'

The idea seemed far less strange than it had only a few days ago when Fiona had received the startling news of who was going to be the locum medical director.

'Hey, Ricky.' Nick leaned towards the frightened young man who was pale and shivering violently beneath his covering of blankets. 'I'm Nick Stewart, one of Lakeview's doctors, and we're going to take good care of you.'

His voice was calm. Confident and reassuring. Yes. She could get used to this.

'I hear you've had a run-in with a pot of boiling oil,' Nick continued sympathetically. 'How's the pain at the moment?'

'I'm c-c-cold...'

'He's had fifteen milligrams of morphine with reasonable effect,' Fiona told Nick. 'The head chef at the restaurant was quick to get him under running cold water and the area had been cooled for a good fifteen minutes by the time we got there.'

'Megan?' Hugh turned to the younger of the two nurses present. 'Could you get some cuddlies, please?'

'Sure.' Eager to respond, Megan brushed past Nick to leave the treatment room. Fiona knew she would be heading for the warming cupboard where the folded, fluffy sheets were kept hot enough to be a real help in warming cold patients. And Ricky *was* cold, which had been an unavoidable complication of treatment thanks to the necessity of cooling the burnt areas of skin for long enough to stop continuing tissue damage. The best that Fiona and Shane had been able to do en route had been to cover him with a foil sheet under the blankets to prevent any further loss of body heat.

'Estimation of area?'

'Maybe eight to ten per cent,' Fiona said. 'No airway involvement. He's been tachycardic at 120, respiratory rate of 30. Blood pressure's been stable at 115 on 75.'

'Let's get another set of vitals as soon as we've transferred him,' Nick said to Lizzie, the nurse manager. Then he turned back to Ricky. 'On a pain scale of one to ten, with one being no pain and ten being the worst you can imagine, what score would you give your pain right now?'

'A...a...f-f-four, I g-guess.'

'We'll do something more about that in just a minute. Hang in there, buddy. You're doing really well.'

It was impossible not to be impressed with Nick's manner. Fiona had seen a lot of doctors in professional settings and she knew that this kind of genuine confidence and warmth could only come from a combination of experience and skill. Even though he was in a totally new hospital with staff and equipment he was not yet familiar with, Nick knew exactly what he was doing and he expected to do it well.

Megan was back with the cuddlies and they put one on the bed before they transferred their patient. Fiona unhooked the oxygen tubing from the portable cylinder and attached it to the overhead supply as the three men in the room lifted Ricky from the stretcher.

Lizzie wrapped a blood-pressure cuff around his arm and put an oxygen saturation monitor probe on his finger. Megan got shears to cut the wet denim from the remains of Ricky's jeans still covering his uninjured leg and pelvic area. Fiona swapped the electrode leads monitoring heart rate and rhythm and then covered the top of Ricky's body with another warmed sheet, but he was still shivering.

'You're still feeling cold, aren't you, Ricky?'

'Y-yes. F-f-freezing…'

Nick looked at the IV cannula Fiona had inserted in Ricky's forearm.

'Still patent?' he queried.

'Should be.'

'Let's start some warmed saline. Megan, could you get that, please?'

'Sure.' But Megan's doubtful expression didn't match her tone.

'Put a bag of saline in the microwave,' Lizzie told her. 'Give it about two minutes.'

'I'll show you,' Hugh offered. 'I should go and check on Wally and see if we've got his angina properly sorted. You happy here, Nick?'

'Absolutely.'

Fiona moved the blankets to cover Ricky's uninjured leg and tucked more around his shoulders. Part of the shivering was due to the shock of the injury and the pain caused but, in a way, Ricky was lucky the injury was so painful. The reassurance Nick was dispensing as he gave their patient a secondary survey to exclude any other injuries was not misplaced.

The only dressing Fiona had applied after cooling the area had been cling film so they could all see the red and blistered skin. If the burns had been full thickness the wounds would have been much darker, even black, and they would have been painless because of nerve destruction. They would also have had no chance of healing without surgery and grafts. He was also lucky there had been no involvement of his face, hands or genital area. Given the depth of the burns, his age and general health, this injury would not be deemed major.

Megan came in with the warmed saline and a dazzling smile for Nick that made Fiona blink. Good grief. Megan was a close friend. They had spent a lot of time together in the last few years but Fiona had never seen her being quite this obvious about being attracted to someone.

'Thanks, Megan. Can you hang that, please?'

'Of course.'

'And, Lizzie, could you draw up some more morphine, please? Let's get Ricky's pain sorted before we think about dressings.'

Hugh returned to the treatment room as Shane left, pushing the stretcher clear with the intention of getting the ambulance tidied and ready for another call. Megan was still busy closing off the IV tubing and then transferring the spike of the giving set to the bag of warmer fluid. Fiona should have been concentrating on completing her paperwork but she was distracted.

Having noticed that smile and then Megan's heightened colour as she attended to the task Nick had requested, she couldn't help watching to find out if she might be reading too much into the non-verbal communication from her friend. Consequently, she was only half listening to the doctors as they discussed a treatment plan for Ricky.

Transfer to a burns unit was not necessary but they would admit him for at least twenty-four hours for observation, pain relief and wound dressing. A tetanus booster would be needed and they were talking about whether prophylactic antibiotics were indicated as Fiona made a new effort to attend to the gaps on her patient report form.

Was Nick as aware as she was of how attracted Megan was to their new staff member? Maybe he was totally oblivious to women that smiled all the time and stole such frequent glances in his direction because it was something that happened all the time.

Fiona had to swallow hard to try and suppress a rather bitter taste in her mouth. Not that she could blame Megan for her reaction to Nick but she had seen it all before, hadn't she? With Al. Women had always thrown themselves in his direction.

'It comes with the territory, babe. It means nothing. Deal with it. And for God's sake, stop taking any notice of the rubbish they put in those tabloids.'

She'd been so naïve. It had taken such a long time to finally lose her trust and she hadn't dealt with it very well at all in the end. Reminders of that miserable period of her life were not exactly something she wanted to have to deal with now either. Not when she had been so confident it was so far behind her it didn't matter any more.

Signing off the increments of morphine she had administered to Ricky, Fiona turned the page to document the trauma area on the body diagrams supplied on the back of the form. A task that would have taken only seconds if she wasn't still distracted.

Megan was seeing Nick fully dressed. Groomed and clean-shaven, although his colouring was dark enough to always have that kind of designer stubble shadow. What would she have thought if she'd run into him early that morning, as she had done when their routes to the bathroom had coincided? With his hair rumpled, his face roughened with definite stubble and an overwhelmingly male body covered only with the boxer shorts and singlet he must have slept in, he had made the size of the villa's wide hallway appear to shrink dramatically.

Megan would probably have simply melted into a

puddle on the carpet, given that the encounter had been enough to give Fiona a very odd internal prickle. Fortunately, it had been easy to dismiss the strange flutter as just an indication that she and Nick needed more time to get used to each other again. To find their way back to the comfortable friendship they'd once had.

Nick had smiled at her this morning.

He had also smiled at Megan when she'd given him the bag of fluids.

Not that she was jealous or anything. That would be ludicrous. Megan was a good few years younger than she was. Probably about Nick's age. She was single and pretty with her auburn hair and green eyes, and she was great company. Ideal girlfriend material, in fact.

Fiona's only vested interest was that she cared about Nick. The way a big sister *should* care. A potential girlfriend would have to be rather special to be good enough. And Megan *was* that special, she told herself firmly. It would be great if the two of them hit it off. Nick might even decide to settle in Queenstown and that way Sam would have his uncle around for years to come.

She should be feeling delighted.

Only she wasn't. Was it just that she felt somehow possessive because Nick qualified as part of her family? She had no right to. It was also nothing to be proud of when she couldn't deny being pleased that there didn't seem to be any return of the sparks Megan was emitting. As arrangements were made to leave Ricky in Lizzie and Megan's capable care for the moment, both Hugh and Nick moved towards the corner bench Fiona was leaning against.

'Nick's pretty well up to speed on our layout and timetables for clinics and visiting consultants,' Hugh said. 'I dragged him through the ward rounds and then I had him on a telephone for half an hour, chasing up progress reports on all the patients we evacuated on Saturday.'

'Oh, good!' Fiona's attention swung to Nick. 'I couldn't see anything much in the papers this morning. What did you find out? Did they end up operating on Claire?'

'The woman with the head injury? No. They've still got her in an induced coma but the intracranial pressure is responding to drug therapy. They're planning another scan and they might lighten sedation later today.'

'And that man you took care of? The one with the chest injury?'

'His name's Ken. He had some pretty major surgery and is still on assisted ventilation in ICU, but it sounds like he's improving as well.'

Fiona liked it that Nick had found out the names of these patients. They were people, not just cases to him and he seemed as pleased to be reporting good news as she was to hear it.

'Your guy with the fractured pelvis, John, is doing really well. He's gone to the orthopaedic ward.'

'And we've discharged the last of the people we kept in for observation,' Hugh added. 'Pretty lucky, really, that there were no fatalities.'

'There could have been, if your emergency services weren't so impressive.'

'Hey, thanks!' Fiona grinned at Nick. 'We like to show off to newcomers, you know.'

'That's good.' Hugh winked at Nick. 'Because my replacement here is free for the rest of the afternoon and he'd like a guided tour of the ambulance facilities at Lakeview.'

'Wouldn't you rather go sightseeing? In that lovely new car you got only yesterday?'

'Sightseeing can wait. I prefer company for that. Someone with lots of local knowledge.'

The sound of laughter drew Fiona's gaze to where Lizzie and Megan were bandaging Ricky's dressings in place. Their patient looked much happier now. He had stopped shivering and must have said something that had made his nurses laugh. Was Megan in contention as a guide? She'd certainly jump at the chance of a ride in the cute little MG sports car Nick had decided to lease despite Fiona's laughing suggestion of a genetic influence.

A firmer mental slap was in order here. Megan was her friend. Nick hadn't really even stepped that close again yet. If he and Megan chose to have a relationship with each other, it was none of her business.

'There's not much to see,' she said. 'You could stay in here and just look out the window.'

'Show me anyway?' Nick's engaging smile would have been enough to persuade anyone. Fiona could almost imagine a sigh coming from Megan's direction. She gave in. Maybe she could drop a hint or two on Megan's behalf.

'Right this way, sir.' She ripped off the top copy of her paperwork and handed it to Hugh. 'You're about to see one of Lakeview Hospital's best-kept secrets.'

'So why is it a secret?'

'Look at it,' Fiona instructed. 'It's old and shabby, cramped and disorganised. If people knew what our base was like, they'd hardly be expecting state-of-the-art pre-hospital medical care, would they?'

Nick was following her from the ambulance bay outside the emergency department across a wide, as-phalted area towards what resembled a large garage that was partially enclosed.

'Does the funding for the ambulance service come out of the hospital's budget?'

'It tops things up if they get too dire. We rely on public donations for the most part, which are, luckily, fairly generous. We're counting on that to continue when we launch a big new campaign later this year for a replacement, purpose-built station. Hugh and Maggie and I have been working on plans and they're really exciting.' Fiona pointed towards the nearby airfield where a bright yellow helicopter stood. 'We managed to acquire that last year, thanks to donations.'

'Pretty impressive. It's a BK711, isn't it? Nice.'

'You know your choppers, then?'

'Yeah. Winch training was one of the first skills I had to get with MSF.'

'Really? Fantastic! That will double the number of winch-trained rescue medics we have available locally at present.'

'Who's the other one?'

'Me.'

'You're kidding!' Nick stopped walking and stared at Fiona.

She raised her chin. 'And why is that so surprising?'

Nick grinned. 'Because you used to get nervous just watching car rallies, and you weren't anywhere near the driver's seat.'

'Maybe that was why,' Fiona countered. 'It can be harder watching someone you love do something dangerous than doing it yourself.'

Nick opened his mouth but then closed it again. Any hint of amusement drained from his face.

'Sorry, Fi. You still miss Al, don't you?'

Fiona swallowed. Should she tell him just how unhappy

the marriage had been in the end? That Sam's conception had been a fluke—the result of an attempted reconciliation they had both known couldn't stand a chance?

'I…I've built a new life,' she said quietly. 'I'm happy, Nick. Very happy.'

But Nick clearly wasn't satisfied. His gaze was curiously intense and the soft touch on her arm underlined the importance of what was on his mind.

'Were you happy with Al?' The question was tentative. Nick must know it might be too soon to step onto such personal ground. 'Was it a good marriage?'

He could see too much. Fiona had to look away and the canary yellow helicopter was as good as anything to focus on. She could see the pilot, Graham Burgess, walking around his beloved machine. He had recognised her from a distance and was waving. Fiona waved back.

'It was a different lifetime,' she said evasively.

Alistair had been Nick's childhood hero. He had told her as much the first time they'd really talked, after that discussion about diabetes. He was now Sam's hero and she wanted her son to grow up being proud of who his father was. To get self-esteem and strength from his family roots.

It had been easy enough to keep an estrangement out of reach of the media because of Al's travel commitments on the international racing circuit and Fiona's career, which had kept her in London for long stretches of time. What would be the point of tarnishing a hero's reputation when it couldn't make any difference other than to hurt people she cared about?

It certainly wouldn't do anything to restore her friendship with Nick and give Sam more time with the only male relative he had. One that he had fallen firmly in love with the moment they had lain on the floor, playing cars together.

'My marriage was wonderful,' she said eventually. Carefully. 'It wasn't real life but it gave me Sam, didn't it? Come on.' She wasn't about to give Nick the opportunity to try and see through the cavernous cracks in her response. 'Let me introduce you to our pilot over there. Graham. He's going to be thrilled to hear you're into winching.'

'I wouldn't say it's my favourite pastime.' Nick took the hint and dropped the personal topic as he followed Fiona. 'More like a necessary evil.'

'Speaking of which...' It was Fiona who stopped their progress this time. She pulled her pager from her belt and read the message. 'Priority one callout,' she relayed. 'To Arrowtown. I'll have to desert you. Sorry, Nick.'

'How come?' Nick was still right beside her as Fiona did an about-turn and quickened her pace. 'I'm having a tour of the ambulance service here, remember? Do you not have room for an observer on board?'

'You want to come for a ride-along?'

'Why not? You seem keen enough for me to dangle out of a chopper to assist you guys. Why not on the ground as well?'

Fiona was heading straight towards the ambulance parked outside the garage. Shane was dragging clear the heavy hose he'd been using to clean the vehicle.

'We good to go?' Fiona queried.

'All set.'

'Cool. We've got a third crew.' Fiona nodded at Nick. 'Jump in, then. There's an extra seat in the back. Put your safety belt on.'

Nick was glad he had followed the instruction.

Fiona drove like a fiend. With the siren wailing, she was

belting along the open road, overtaking cars and tourist buses and barely slowing for curves on the road.

A lightning-fast glance at their extra passenger must have revealed how nervous he was feeling because Fiona laughed.

'Maggie taught me high-speed driving,' she shouted over the noise of the siren. 'Plus, I must have picked up a bit by osmosis from Al.'

Shane certainly seemed astonishingly relaxed. His body leaned with the roll of the speeding vehicle and he was managing to consult a map at the same time.

'It's one of those little streets off the main drag. We turn right just after that restaurant in the old post office building.'

'What are we going to?' Nick called.

'Unconscious person. Could be anything.'

Much to Nick's relief, Fiona slowed the vehicle markedly as they entered the small historic settlement of Arrowtown, several miles north of Queenstown. She also turned the siren off but the glow of the beacons in the fading afternoon light was enough to clear their path of any traffic or dawdling pedestrians.

'Pretty place,' Fiona said unnecessarily. 'You'll have to come and explore it properly some time, Nick. Down here, Shane?'

'Yeah. Look, there's someone waving.'

The 'someone' turned out to be a neighbour.

'I heard this huge crash,' he told the ambulance crew as they pulled a stretcher from the back of the truck and loaded it with gear. 'Breaking glass and stuff. I called out but when I got no answer I went to have a look and I found him just lying out there by his rubbish bin.'

Fiona dropped to a crouch in a sea of rubbish and broken glass as they reached the crumpled figure. She shook his shoulder.

'Hello, can you hear me? Hullo!'

There was no response. Shane moved in to help her roll the man over.

'Careful with his neck,' Fiona cautioned. 'And watch out for the broken glass.'

'Hey, I know this guy,' Nick said in surprise, as the man's face came into view. 'It's Jeff, isn't it?'

'Yeah,' the neighbour confirmed. 'Jeff Smythe.'

Fiona had her fingers on the man's neck, checking for a pulse. She raised her eyebrows at Nick.

'That cast on his hand,' he explained. 'He's one of the people we treated on Saturday. He lost a finger and broke another one.'

'I remember.' Fiona nodded. 'His camera got caught on the car and the strap must have been wound around his fingers.'

'Looks like he might have broken the cast as well.' Shane shifted his gaze having checked their patient's airway.

'Good pulse,' Fiona commented. Her nose wrinkled as she straightened to look around her.

Nick had noticed more than the smell of old rubbish as well. 'Could be those broken bottles,' he suggested.

'Hmmm.' Fiona rubbed her knuckles on the man's sternum. 'Jeff? Open your eyes,' she said loudly. 'Wake up!'

The man groaned and tried to roll over again, beginning to vomit as he did so. The smell of alcohol increased sharply.

'He's drunk,' the neighbour noted in disgust. 'Sorry. I wouldn't have called you if I didn't think there was something really wrong with him.'

'He still needs help,' Fiona said mildly. She supported Jeff on his side until he stopped vomiting. 'Does he live alone?'

Jeff rolled onto his back again. His eyes opened briefly and he mumbled incoherently. Fiona slipped an oxygen mask onto his face.

'He had a girlfriend but I got the impression she took off a couple of days ago.'

Right after his injury? Nick frowned. 'He was really upset at losing his finger,' he remembered. 'He reckoned his career was over.' Had he missed something important in his patient contact that day? It had been pressured and exhausting but that was no excuse. He'd known that Jeff needed support. He'd just assumed that the girlfriend who was coming to collect him would provide it. Maybe he should have spent more time talking to this man.

'I don't think this cast was broken by his fall.' Shane was examining Jeff's lower arm. 'It's dented and cracked all over the place, like he was hitting something.'

'I'll check his limb baselines,' Fiona decided aloud, as she pulled the leads from the side pocket of the life pack. 'Have a quick look inside, Shane. We'd better make sure we're not dealing something more than an ETOH overdose.'

Nick had a look at Jeff's hand while Fiona was attaching the electrodes that would enable them to monitor heart rhythm and rate.

'Capillary refill isn't great on the broken finger,' he reported. 'And the hand's really cold. And dirty.'

Shane returned with two bottles of tablets in his hand.

'They're the antibiotics and painkillers we discharged him with,' Nick said. He opened the bottles as Shane helped Fiona with a quick set of baseline recordings. 'Painkillers are gone,' he told them. 'But he hasn't taken any of the ABs.'

'Let's get him on the stretcher. It's too cold to hang

around out here.' Fiona smiled at the neighbour. 'Thanks for your help,' she said. 'Would you be able to lock the house up and keep an eye on things for Jeff?'

'I guess.' But the man sounded dubious. 'It's not his house, though. He just rents it.'

Fiona continued talking to the neighbour as Shane and Nick moved the stretcher closer.

'Jeff's been through a fair bit in the last few days,' she said. 'Not everybody copes that well when things get too much.'

The neighbour nodded. 'I didn't know he was that badly hurt. I thought he'd just broken his wrist or something.'

Fiona stood up and moved the life pack and oxygen cylinder to allow the men to lift Jeff onto the stretcher. She was watching their patient carefully, Nick noted, and the frown on her face suggested focus, not judgment of any kind. She seemed oblivious to the unpleasant setting and smell around them and certainly wasn't compromising her standard of care because this crisis had been self-inflicted.

Nick could feel a kind of inward nod. Of both approval and confirmation. He'd always suspected she'd be like this in a professional environment and it didn't seem that long ago that he had wished he *could* see it. Back when he'd been envious that that had been how Al had met Fiona in the first place—when he'd been injured in a rally crash and she'd been on duty in the ED he'd been taken to.

Now he could not only observe this woman at work, he could work alongside her.

As an unexpected bonus of a new job, this one would sure take some beating.

It was three days before Jeff was allowed to go back to his home in Arrowtown.

The day after that was Saturday and Nick and Fiona had also come back to Arrowtown, this time with Sam.

They had walked down the main street, admiring the old buildings and galleries and the abundant reminders that this had been a gold-mining settlement.

'My legs are tired, Mummy,' Sam announced as they reached the end of their route beside the old post office restaurant.

'Lunch?' Nick suggested.

'Let's get some sandwiches and drinks at one of the cafés. I've got somewhere else I really want to show you today while the weather's this good. You're going to be busy moving into the Patterson place tomorrow. And, besides, I have a sneaking suspicion this might be where Bernie is taking Mum for lunch. I wouldn't want her to think I was checking up on them.'

Nick ruffled Sam's hair. 'Would those tired legs like a piggyback?'

'Yes!'

Nick lifted the small boy onto the top of the stone wall beside the footpath and then turned and bent down so that Sam could wrap his arms around his neck and his legs around his waist. Fiona was looking at the nearby street.

'I wonder how Jeff's getting on?'

'He was in much better shape when I talked to him on the ward yesterday. Brilliant idea of yours, asking him to work on the publicity for the new fundraising campaign. He's going to give it a good shot, I think.'

'We were looking for someone. Seemed like a win-win situation.'

'There's not many people that would go out of their way for a patient like that. I'm impressed.'

Fiona just smiled. It would have been worth doing just to get an appreciative glance like that from Nick.

'He's got a few issues going on,' Nick continued more cautiously. 'Don't let him get too dependent on you, Fi.'

'I won't.'

'Good. Now, where's this place you're taking me next?'

'It's a surprise.'

'It's more than a surprise. It's magic, that's what it is.'

'Gorgeous, isn't it?'

'It's *real*!'

'Sure is.' But Fiona wasn't looking at the spectacular scenery in front of them. Or even at Sam, who was running from tree to tree in the forest, pretending to hide but unable to stay put for more than thirty seconds at a time.

She was watching Nick as he turned an incredulous gaze back to the towering, snow-capped peaks behind them, to the glimpse of the river and the sweep of the untouched wilderness bordering the forest.

The expression on his face was compelling. A grownup version of the kind of wonder Sam displayed whenever the boundaries of his small world suddenly expanded. Nick was right. It *was* magic and knowing that she had been the one to bestow this gift gave Fiona the warmest glow.

Not that it had been difficult. All she had done had been to drive Nick less than an hour away from Queenstown, not counting the stop for a picnic lunch, to the Glenorchy region at the head of Lake Wakatipu. An area now famous for its role in providing beautiful fantasy settings for movies. The kind of excursion it was easy to offer any guest. His rapt appreciation of their destination meant that it had been exactly the right thing to do, however, and the mutual pleasure was bringing them closer together again.

Unravelling the final kinks in that knot that had lain between them over the last week.

'*This* was why I came to New Zealand,' he said solemnly.

'For a fantasy set tour? You're a movie buff?'

'No.' Nick took a deep breath that was released in a sigh. 'It goes a lot deeper than that.'

'A lot deeper,' he repeated a minute later as they started walking again, by tacit consent, following Sam's erratic path through the forest.

It seemed an invitation to talk about something more personal but Sam was running back towards them right now, his face alight with excitement.

'Mummy! I'm going on a *bear* hunt!'

'Are you, sweetheart?'

'Yes. I'm in the *forest*!'

'I didn't think New Zealand had any bears,' Nick said.

'We don't. Sam's just acting out one of his favourite stories.'

'It doesn't involve his dad, does it? Hunting bears?'

Fiona laughed. 'No, this one comes from a book. Didn't you notice the books Sam has in his room? Some of them are falling apart because we read them so often.'

'I was like that. Only I had to wait until I was old enough to start reading for myself.'

'Really?' Fiona was shocked. 'Didn't your mother ever read to you in bed?'

Nick shook his head. 'I think she used up whatever maternal urges she had on Al. They called me an after-thought but I always knew they really meant a mistake. Al was old enough to look after himself by the time I came along and Mum's life was full of far more exciting things by then than staying home with a baby.'

'That's really sad.' Again, Fiona was struck by how

little she knew of Nick's childhood, but this was worse than not knowing he'd had asthma. How could any mother let their child grow up feeling 'invisible'? She had to resist the urge to touch Nick. To let him know that she sympathised.

More than sympathised. This was a side of Nick that touched something deep in her. Vulnerable was too pathetic a word for a man who exuded the kind of inner strength Nick did. It was more that he was prepared to reveal something so personal. Al had been like that at the beginning. When he had been injured. Had that been reason she had fallen in love with him? The thought was startling. It took a moment to refocus on what Nick was saying.

'I didn't miss what I never had, I guess. But when I learned to read I found that there really *was* magic in the world.' Nick's step slowed after his sidelong glance at Fiona. 'Why are you smiling?'

'It's the second time you've mentioned magic.'

'You find that strange?'

'Well, you're a doctor. A scientist. Most doctors I know wouldn't admit to believing in magic.'

'Maybe they didn't read fantasy books when they were ten.' Nick's laugh was self-effacing. 'A few more times after that, in fact. It was like a security blanket. A place to escape that worked well enough to feel like magic.'

Fiona grinned. 'Magic?'

'Amazing, anyway. Too good to be true. A bit like finding you and discovering I have a real-life nephew. Family...'

'Speaking of which...' Fiona's head turned swiftly. 'Sam? Where are you?'

The silence was unnerving. For a horrible moment

Fiona thought she might have been so caught up in listening to Nick and enjoying the feeling that they'd reconnected that she'd allowed her only child to get lost.

Nick touched her arm. A gentle grip that gave a surprising sensation of strength. He tilted his head and rolled his eyes. The movement was subtle but enough for Fiona to spot the toe of a small shoe protruding from the mossy base of a treetrunk.

'Boo!'

Sam hurtled into his mother's arms. 'You didn't see me, did you, Mummy? I gave you a *fright*, didn't I?'

'You sure did,' Fiona said with conviction. She caught Nick's gaze over the top of Sam's head. His face was solemn but his dark eyes were smiling and she could swear she still felt the touch of his hand.

It was a feeling of reassurance.

Of safety.

Of being with someone who had understood completely.

Someone who cared.

And it felt *so* good.

Fiona needed to find a way of sharing how good it felt—preferably one that didn't involve pulling Nick into some kind of cheesy group hug.

'Do you think it's too cold to go and find an ice cream somewhere?'

'No!' Sam said.

'Definitely not,' Nick agreed.

'Come on, then.' Fiona put Sam down but kept hold of his hand. The little boy casually held out his other hand and just as casually, Nick took hold of it.

The three of them walked out of the forest and Fiona had the weirdest feeling that Sam was like an extension of both herself and Nick. He was their link. A son and a nephew.

That might explain why the connection was strong enough to make her feel like she was actually holding hands with Nick. And why it felt like the most natural thing in the world to *be* doing.

He may not realise it yet but Nick Stewart belonged there.

CHAPTER SIX

IT WAS too easy to feel like he belonged there.

Things were falling into place for Nick with a strange kind of inevitability, like the combinations on the lock of a safe tumbling from one correct alignment to the next. A process that could be leading to a secure, heavy door swinging open. Entry to a place Nick had never been so he had no idea what could be behind that door.

The first click of those tumblers finding a correct position had been meeting Fiona again, of course—along with the discovery of his nephew and the closest thing to a family Nick had ever known.

The second had been falling in love with *where* he was, thanks to that trip Fiona had taken him on last weekend. And maybe another turn of that lock had also been discovered on that outing. Sharing that magic had been enough to reconnect. To uncover the bond of friendship he had originally had with Fiona. Except that this felt new. Stronger. Tempered by maturity and the reminder that it was perfectly possible to turn on a force field that could direct any inappropriate emotions inward and make them undetectable to anyone else. He'd learned those skills way back, hadn't he? Learned that it was better to make the most of what you had and not hanker after things you could never have.

And, just in case that hadn't been enough, fate had shifted him into the Patterson household. A month felt semi-permanent thanks to the almost nomadic life Nick had led for years, and this dwelling and its setting had to be the most beautiful place in the world. Hugh had converted a long, low structure that had once been shearers' quarters and the house sat only a stone's throw from the vast and rather mysterious waters of Lake Wakatipu.

Fiona had told him a version of the Maori legend in which a terrible sleeping giant had been set on fire. The snow and ice on the surrounding mountains had been melted by the heat and the run-off had been enough to fill an eighty-kilometre length of valleys. The giant was still there and this was why the lake apparently 'breathed' with a rhythmical rise and fall of its water level every five minutes.

There was, no doubt, a scientific explanation for this phenomenon. It probably had something to do with one point being the deepest in any southern hemisphere lake or the fact that its icy temperature barely changed between summer and winter, but Nick rather liked the magic and mystery of the legend.

Fantasy.

Escape.

Tucked under the shadow of the Remarkables—a towering, bleak mountain range—with the lake opposite and an expanse of farmland on either side, it should have been a lonely place to live for someone used to sharing close, makeshift quarters with large groups of people, but Nick was far from lonely.

He had Hugh and Maggie's two old sheepdogs, Tuck

and Lass, to keep him company and encourage him to walk the stony shores of the lake every day and soak in the beauty. With the Murchisons on the other side of that lake, he had family to visit whenever he felt the need and, only partly due to Sam's insistence, Nick had already clocked up two visits in the five days since he'd moved. Close, but not too close. The force field could be turned off and its energy levels restored far more easily with a little distance.

He also had a working environment that was different enough to be a novelty and varied enough to keep him interested. And he had the added bonus of Fiona being virtually a colleague. The ambulance station was just a few steps away from the hospital and it was a journey that was becoming a habit despite the fact that Nick was only approaching the end of his first week as Lakeview's medical director.

It was a journey he was making again now and Nick paused on finding Shane about to begin his usual end-of-day vehicle clean.

'You doing anything tonight?'

'Nothing special. Why?'

'I'm shouting pizza and a few drinks at the Fox and Hound down the road. Steve and Lizzie and Megan are coming. I was hoping you and Fi might like to come as well.'

'Sounds good to me. What's the occasion?'

'Getting to the end of my first week working here.' Nick grinned. 'Oh, yeah…it's also my birthday.'

'Hey! Many happy returns, mate!'

'Thanks. Fi inside?'

'Yeah. She's been showing that guy around. Jeff. The one who's getting involved in the fundraising campaign?'

Nick nodded. 'I know him.'

'They were heading for the storeroom when I came out. Jeff wanted to see what sort of supplies we keep on station.'

Nick could hear Fiona before he saw her. As he stepped into the garage he wasn't far away from the open door of the storeroom. He stopped, not wanting to interrupt the conversation. He wasn't in a hurry and it was hardly a hardship to listen to the sound of Fiona's voice and let his imagination play with what she looked like.

'Traction splints...' he heard. 'Used for broken femurs. They're less painful and the patient loses less blood if they're splinted properly.'

Nick could imagine the way Fiona was using her hands as she spoke. Supple joints and long fingers in a kind of graceful dance of emphasis.

'There's a heap of stuff in here.'

'It looks a lot because it's crammed into a small space but we do get a lot of trauma. Much more than your average city station would get.'

'Why is that?' Jeff sounded interested. Keen.

'Nature of the place,' Fiona responded. 'We're one of the world's favourite adventure playgrounds. We've got skiing, mountain climbing, white-water rafting, bungee-jumping, jet-boating...' Was she counting the sports off on her fingers? 'You name it, if it's fast or dangerous, it'll be happening somewhere around here.'

Nick found himself smiling. He knew that Fiona's hazel eyes would be shining as she spoke. He could hear the passion she had for her career. People would be out there doing their adventure sports and inevitably some would be injuring themselves. Fiona and her colleagues would be ready and more than willing to get to the top of a mountain or the bottom of a canyon to rescue them.

'Yeah. Guess I've had first-hand experience of that, haven't I?'

'This is one of our scoop stretchers over here. Good for getting people out of awkward places. Like the hunters that seem to get shot or injured at regular intervals. How is your hand, by the way?'

'A lot better, thanks.' Jeff's voice got suddenly quieter. 'I'm really sorry about last week. You know…I've never done anything like that before.'

'Forget it. We all have our moments.'

'I just don't want you thinking I'm some kind of loser. I was freaked out, losing my finger, you know? My girlfriend walking out didn't help either.'

'She walked out because you lost your finger?' Fiona sounded shocked. Kind of the way she'd sounded on learning that Nick's mother had never read him stories. Was she looking at Jeff the way she'd looked at him? With that soft, sympathetic expression? Nick straightened from where he'd been leaning on the wall, watching Shane hose down the ambulance. He hoped she wasn't.

'Nah, it hadn't been going anywhere anyway. Me being down about my hand was just the last straw, I guess.'

'You'll get through it.' Fiona sounded encouraging now.

'I've certainly got a good reason to try.'

Nick started walking towards the storeroom. Did Jeff mean the job he'd been given to help with the fundraising campaign or was he talking about Fiona's company?

Just why was he making a point about his single status?

A bubble of a nasty emotion formed in his gut. *So* familiar. The green-eyed monster—jealousy. Nick knew he'd better intensify that force field before he stepped into that storeroom or he might do something incredibly stupid, like punch Jeff on the nose.

It wouldn't be the first time something like that had happened.

The memory threatened to switch the force field off completely. Instead of interrupting the couple still in the storeroom, Nick turned on his heel and strode through the office area and into the staff toilet. He turned on the cold tap, filled his cupped hands and splashed his face.

He repeated the action. The third time he simply held his hands to his face, letting the water dribble through his fingers, his breath coming out in a forceful whoosh as he tried to blow the memories away.

The night of his brother's stag party.

The night before Al had married Fiona.

Nick had been twenty. Still a medical student. Still no more than the gawky teenager who could have been a pin-up model for the guy who got sand kicked in his face at the beach. A slightly taller version of the kid who had got asthma from petrol fumes. The family embarrassment.

Stickman, Al had called him.

He'd grown up faster than his family had realised, though. On the inside, anyway.

He understood things like responsibility. Commitment. Morality.

A few beers at the stag party provided more than enough Dutch courage when it became obvious that the stripper engaged for entertainment was going to get lucky and spend the rest of the night with the famous sports star.

The confrontation took place in the restroom of that hotel. Beside basins that looked remarkably like the one Nick was currently gripping as he stared into the mirror.

It wasn't his face he was seeing. All it required was a bit of a squint and he could see Alistair staring back. With that incredulous expression resulting from Nick's appalled accusation.

'You've got no intention of being faithful to Fi, have you?' he'd demanded.

'I've got every intention of living my life the way I want to, thanks very much.'

'Why *are* you marrying Fi, Al?'

'Why not? She's cute. She adores me. I adore her.' He'd laughed. 'I'm in a high-risk game. I'm bound to need my private nurse again.'

'You "*adore*" her? And you'd still sleep with someone you don't even know the night before your *wedding*? You make me sick.'

'Ooh! Who made you the moral police, Stickman?'

'You're a bastard, Al. You can't even see how wrong it is. Have you got any idea how much it would hurt Fi if she knew? Do you actually *care*?'

'Why should *you* care? Oh-h, you fancy her, don't you?' And Alistair had laughed again. The memory of that nasty sound was still enough to make the hairs on the back of Nick's neck prickle. 'What a joke! Listen, mate, your only claim to fame will ever be the fact that you're related to me. You think someone like Fi would ever look at someone like you? Get *real*, kiddo.'

The shove had been dismissive, just a physical put-down to emphasise the hurtful words, but it had been the last straw. Nick had shoved back in an attempt to stand his ground. Maybe it had been the notion that if *he* wasn't strong enough to make his point then Fi stood no chance.

The marriage was doomed and Fiona deserved so much better.

Alistair had won the fight, of course. Just like he'd always won everything. Nick had ended up with a black eye and a mild concussion, feeling sick as he stood beside his brother in the church the following day, knowing that his physical symptoms were only partly due to the blows he'd taken.

Nick dried his face and headed for the door. He shouldn't feel any of that old guilt. The marriage had been wonderful, hadn't it? Maybe Fiona had never found out.

He couldn't have told her at the time, could he? She wouldn't have believed him and the only thing he would have achieved would have been to spoil a perfect day for her. A wedding fit for royalty with wall-to-wall cameras waiting to record the joy on her face.

The smug satisfaction on Alistair's face.

The black eye that make-up had only partially covered on the face of the best man.

'Best man?' Al had managed a final jibe after a few glasses of champagne at the reception. One of the last times Nick had spoken to his brother, in fact. 'What a joke. We both know who the best man is, don't we Nicholas?' The grin had been one of pure triumph. 'The *best* man won, didn't he?'

'Nick, hi!'

Fiona hoped her welcoming tone and smile didn't convey too much relief but she was delighted by his appearance in her office. Jeff had been standing just a little too close to her as she had been showing him the maps on the wall and the area the ambulance service covered. It was making her feel uneasy.

The rumble of Shane driving the ambulance into the garage beside them meant that the office was going to be even more crowded any minute.

'You got enough for now, Jeff?'

'Yeah. Thanks. I like your idea of using real people and stories to get the point across about how vital the service is. You get some exciting rescues.'

'We don't want to focus only on the dramatic stuff, mind you. There are far more people who rely on us for the majority of our work. Medical crises like heart attacks and asthma and diabetes and stokes and so on.'

'So you'll find people I can talk to?'

'As soon as I get a spare minute or three.' Fiona walked to the office door and Jeff seemed happy to take the hint and leave.

Or maybe not. He was taking a good look at the cluttered desk he was passing. And then he paused, leaning in to admire the picture of Sam that took pride of place beside the telephone.

'Cute kid.'

'That's Sam,' Fiona said proudly. 'My son.'

'And my nephew,' Nick added. He had his arms folded and the look he was giving Jeff was distinctly cool. If it hadn't been a crazy thought, Fiona would have considered it challenging.

'Oh?' Jeff's quick glance went from Nick to Fiona and back again. She could almost see the wheels turning as he tried to figure out what their relationship was. Leaving him puzzled might not be a bad thing, she decided, given that uncomfortable feeling of proximity she'd just experienced. Her private life was not part of the available information package.

'Why don't I give you a call next week?' she said briskly. 'When I've had the chance to chase up some contacts.'

'Sure.' Jeff was really leaving this time. He flicked another glance at Nick and then smiled at Fiona. 'Call me any time.'

Shane was whistling cheerfully in the garage as he completed packing up for the day. He waved at Jeff and then poked his head into the office.

'See you guys down the road later, then. I'm going to duck home and get changed.'

'Down the road?' Fiona queried.

'Nick's shouting everybody, didn't he tell you yet? It's his birthday.'

Fiona rounded on Nick as Shane headed home. 'Why didn't you *tell* me? Oh, I feel awful! I haven't got you a present or a card or…anything. And it must be…your thirtieth, isn't it? That's special!'

'It's no big deal.' Nick's tone was reassuring. 'Look, I've been known to forget my own birthday at times with the weird places I've been living in. And I've always hated parties and fuss. It was just a last-minute idea to have a few drinks. Think of it more as me wanting to get to know my temporary colleagues a bit better.'

'No way. I'll get you a present tomorrow. You'll have to come home for dinner so we can have a family celebration. Sam *loves* parties! And, hey!' Fiona stepped close and threw her arms around Nick. 'Happy birthday!'

She kissed him.

The way you would offer a kiss to any family member or friend on their special day. She aimed for his cheek, of course, or maybe the corner of his mouth, but Nick moved to return the hug and his face moved and the kiss moved all at the same time.

And Fiona found her lips touching Nick's.

Just briefly. Softly.

It shouldn't have meant anything.

It certainly shouldn't have had the effect of a bomb going off. Nerve endings exploding into an electrifying jolt. Fiona stepped back quickly. So quickly she almost overbalanced, given that Nick let her go instantly.

Cover it up, her instincts screamed. Bury it. At least *hide* it!

So she laughed. 'Whoops! Better not do that when I've had a glass of wine or two, had I?'

No wonder Nick was giving her a strange look. Bemused, even.

Distraction was a good ploy. 'I'll follow Shane's example and go home and get changed.' Did it sound like she was babbling? 'What time is everybody getting there?'

'About seven.'

'Great. The night-shift volunteers will be taking over in half an hour or so, which will just give me time to get sorted.' The papers on her desk didn't really need shuffling but Fiona had to do *something*.

'I'll go and get the dogs fed and watered.' Nick's look was cautious as he moved to the door. 'See you later, then.'

'Absolutely.' Fiona gave Nick the brightest smile she could summon.

A smile that faded the instant he walked out.

She sat down at her desk. Buried her face in her hands and, finally, allowed herself to face the internal havoc her body was still buzzing with.

The realisation that she was attracted to Nick was as unexpected as it was undesirable. This was no simple appreciation of an extremely good-looking man. Neither was it a result of the warmth you could get from a good friendship.

This was…*huge*.

The first time Fiona had felt like this in…

Oh, Lord—it felt like the first time she had *ever* felt like this.

She would just have to deal with it. Hide it. Make damned sure Nick didn't guess.

There was no harm in making a little extra effort to look good for going out, though, was there?

Not that anyone got really dressed up to go to the Hound but her black jeans fitted well and looked good.

Sexy...

The top with diamanté on its deep scooped neckline might be a tad over the top but this was a special occasion.

'Is it really Uncle Nick's birthday, Mummy?'

'It sure is.'

'Why can't I come to the party?'

'It's not really a party tonight. And it's just for grown-ups.'

'Will there be balloons?'

'No.'

'A cake? With candles?'

'No. We can have those tomorrow night. We'll need to buy some candles.'

'How many?'

'Thirty. Do you know how many thirty is, sweetheart?'

'No. Is it lots?'

'Heaps.' But not as many as Fiona would need. Even if she'd met Nick with no history between them, he wouldn't be interested. He was Shane's age, for goodness' sake, and Shane's girlfriend was twenty-five.

Fiona was thirty-six. An older woman. A much older woman. And why was she even thinking about the difference in their ages, anyway?

'Is Ga going?'

'No. She's staying home with you.' Fiona decided to leave her hair loose. It wasn't that it made her look younger or anything. It was just more festive. She brushed it until it shone and then slipped on a thin silver headband to hold it back from her face. 'She's going to bake the cake for tomorrow and you can help.'

'What sort of cake?'

'Chocolate.'

'Do I get to lick the spoon?'

'Of course.' Fiona scooped Sam up for a cuddle. 'That's the best bit, isn't it?'

Nick had to lick the string of melted cheese off his fingers but nobody seemed to notice his lack of table manners.

The group of Lakeview Hospital's staff were crammed into a corner booth of a pub that was doing its best to look like a bit of Olde England, with its crackling open fire, heavy exposed beams and solid, dark furniture. The homely smell of hot food masked a faint hint of stale beer and the laughter, animated conversation and camaraderie of the group made it a good place to be.

Fiona was having trouble with the cheese as well. She caught the long string dangling from her slice of pizza and put her tongue out to catch it.

A shaft of desire powerful enough to take his breath away came from nowhere to twist Nick's gut.

He couldn't look away. Could barely hear the sound of Megan's voice from right beside him.

'So how old *are* you today, Nick?'

'Thirty. Really ancient.'

Fiona had caught him staring at her mouth. Now *she* was staring back at *him*.

'What exotic Third World location did you have your last birthday party in?'

'I don't do parties.' He never had. Not since that awful

night when the glow surrounding the hero of his childhood had been irreparably tarnished. People drank too much at parties. Did things they later regretted. Or *should* regret.

'*This* is a party,' Fiona said. She was still holding eye contact and her smile was soft. 'Happy birthday, Nick.'

'Yes! Happy birthday,' everyone chorused.

'Thanks.' Nick *had* to tear his gaze away from Fiona before he started looking like an idiot. He managed but he knew the success wouldn't last for long.

God knew, he was trying but it was a losing battle tonight. It had been a struggle ever since Fiona had walked into the Hound looking like she'd poured those long legs into the dark jeans, with the sparkle of little jewels on her neckline making the creamy flesh above them an irresistible visual target and her hair flowing down her back like black silk.

Nick wanted to grab a fistful of that hair. To wind it around his hand until Fiona's head was caught and tilted to just the right angle. To feel her lips against his. Not the brush of a butterfly's wing kind of kiss that she'd given him in her office today.

A *real* kiss.

'I wonder where you'll be celebrating your next birthday,' Lizzie said.

'No idea,' Nick said lightly. 'I haven't resigned from MSF yet so I could get deployed anywhere, any time, as soon as I've finished this locum.'

'Don't you get sick of travelling?' Megan asked. 'Wouldn't you like to settle down somewhere?'

'Yeah.' Shane raised his glass of beer in a toast. 'Thirty's getting on, mate. Might be time to start thinking about putting down some roots.'

Nick just smiled. Shane didn't need to know it was much safer not to put down roots. That way, they couldn't get ripped up. He'd be gone from this place in a few short weeks and that was probably just as well, the way he was feeling tonight. Just how long could a force field last?

He caught Fiona's glance again. The lighting in this pub was extremely dim. He could actually imagine something in her gaze reflecting the way *he* was feeling.

Man, it was too hot in here with that blazing fire. Nick could feel the thud of his pulse as his heart rate increased.

'This isn't a bad place to live,' Lizzie was saying. 'You might want to think about it, Nick.'

'Yes.' Megan sounded encouraging. 'We'd love you to stay.'

'Sam must be loving having a real uncle around,' Shane put in. 'Is that right, Fi?'

'He sure is.'

'Must be almost like having his dad here.' Shane grinned. 'Or didn't you two look much alike, Nick?'

'I was better-looking.' It was easy not to catch Fiona's eye this time. He didn't want to see confirmation that his presence was welcome because he was a replacement for his brother. 'Your medical director will be back in town in no time,' he added. 'You don't need two of them.'

'We could do with a surgeon, though,' Lizzie said. 'Didn't you say you'd like to do more than your basic training in general surgery?'

'One day, yes. But it won't be here.'

'Why not?' Steve came back with a tray of new drinks for everybody. 'We've got great facilities. We just can't use them for anything more than minor stuff.'

'Jenny would be keen,' Fiona said.

'Who's Jenny?'

'One of our GPs. She trained in anaesthetics, thinking she'd be able to use the skills here at least part time.'

'So why don't you advertise for a surgeon?'

'Logistics,' Fiona said. 'The case load isn't enough. It's more effective to fly patients to larger hospitals and you'd have to do that for anything major anyway. Mind you, it *would* be great to have someone with the skills to stabilise critical cases before we evacuated them.'

'Sounds like a job for someone ready to retire.'

'Or someone who wanted something really different. A job with lots of variety.'

'Someone like you,' Megan offered. 'You must do a bit of everything in war zones and places like that.'

'True.'

For a while they quizzed Nick on his work with MSF and then the conversation shifted and they talked about Steve's interest in rock climbing and diving and Shane's determination to learn to ski this year. Megan was enthusiastic about dance classes she'd started but Nick was only half listening.

What would it be like to stay? he wondered. To get to see Sam grow up? To be in a position to be a father figure instead of a distant uncle?

Heart-breaking, that's what it would be.

He made the next trip to the bar, having persuaded Fiona to have another glass of wine with the offer to drive her home.

What had he been thinking?

He'd be alone, in a small car, with the sexiest woman he'd ever seen. One that was looking at him strangely tonight. For the second time, when he handed her the glass and their fingers touched, Nick thought he saw an echo of his own desire in her eyes.

It *was* possible. He had to remind her of Al every time she looked at him. Especially in an atmosphere like this.

Al had always been surrounded by crowds. People dressed up and drinking and partying the night away. He'd always been the centre of attention.

The way he had been tonight.

Yes. It was possible that he reminded Fiona of Al enough for Nick to get a lot closer to her if he tried.

As close as he wanted to get. Physically, anyway.

It wouldn't be *him* she wanted, of course. He'd be a replacement.

But if that got him to the place he'd always wanted to be, did it really matter?

The temptation was strong. If felt like another click of those tumblers getting very close to falling into place.

He could shake them and make sure it didn't happen.

Or not.

For a long time the ride home was quiet.

Fiona felt very close to the ground in Nick's little sports car. It gave an illusion of speed that was probably not justified. Or was that coming from the amount of wine she'd had tonight? Far more than she might normally but it had been hard work to try and keep things normal. To make sure she didn't scare Nick back to the other side of the world.

Lizzie's comment tonight had fed the seed of an idea Fiona hadn't been allowing to take root, but what if Nick *did* decide he'd like to stay?

How wonderful would that be?

She stole another glance at the profile of the man beside her. His face was relaxed, his hands resting lightly on the steering-wheel. He was in control. So close that Fiona could feel the warmth of his body. Could smell a hint of something too subtle and too masculine to be a commercial aftershave. Something unique.

The smell of Nick.

'Have I got some pizza stuck to my ear or something?'

Fiona laughed. 'No. Why?'

'You keep looking at me.'

'Do I?' Oh, help! She wasn't very good at hiding things after all. 'I…I guess it's been a long time since I got driven home after a night out. It feels…kind of weird.'

Nick thought about that for a minute.

'Weird strange or weird nice?' he asked as he pulled to a halt near the Murchisons' gate, which was screened from the lights of the house by a thick hedge. When he flicked the car's headlights off, the world outside was swallowed by darkness. Then he just sat, smiling. Waiting patiently for a response from his passenger.

'Weird nice,' Fiona said finally. Her eyes were readjusting to the change in light as she unclipped her safety belt. Maybe the wine was responsible for more than the sense of speed. It seemed to be making it far easier to hold Nick's gaze.

'Nice' didn't begin to explain how she felt but, given that the feeling was due to her attraction to Nick, she could hardly try and define it better, could she?

A part of her she'd forgotten existed seemed to have come alive again tonight. Or had that happened in her office a little earlier?

For the last five years she had existed only within the roles of being a daughter and a mother and, more recently, as a paramedic. Tonight she'd had an hour or two of being simply herself.

A woman. One that was in the company of a very desirable man.

Alive was the word for it all right. Her senses felt reborn. Sharpened.

'I don't mind,' Nick said. 'I think I like it.'

Fiona said nothing. Her heightened sense of hearing was playing with the sound of his voice. Letting it trickle over her like a cool breeze on the hottest of summer days.

'Like what?' she asked belatedly, as she noticed the silence.

'You looking at me.'

'Oh…' His smile was perfect. Slow and easy. Just… Nick. She couldn't help smiling back. 'I think I like it, too.'

'Like what?'

'Looking at you.'

It was a silly conversation but Nick laughed and the soft sound was joyous. Fiona felt absurdly pleased for giving him a reason to laugh. Her smile widened.

'Happy birthday, Nick.'

Was it an excuse for another kiss? Or was it an invitation?

A second later, it didn't matter. Nick leaned towards her and the touch of his lips felt suddenly familiar.

Like coming home.

For a moment Fiona revelled in the feeling of safety. Of being held so gently against the warm strength of a large male body. She could feel the slide of Nick's hands into her hair and even hear the squeak of his leather jacket as he pulled her closer.

And then she was aware of nothing but his mouth. The sensation of his lips and, dear God, his *tongue*. Fiona was sucked into that kiss so deeply she could have drowned and she wouldn't have cared.

It was the most amazing kiss.

Stunning.

When it ended Fiona had to consciously close her mouth and stop gaping.

'Oh, my God,' she whispered. *'Nick?'*

His voice was oddly rough. 'That's me.'

'What *was* that?'

'Just a kiss, hon.'

'But…' It was a kiss that was not supposed to happen. Now Nick would know how she felt. The dawning re-alisation was a wake-up call. Fiona drew back, horrified with herself. She had been kissing Nick.

Sam's uncle.

Al's brother.

'Yeah…' Nick cleared his throat. He sat up straighter. 'It *was* a bit different, wasn't it? Magic, even.'

'Um…' What was that supposed to mean, *a bit different*? Was that good or really bad? 'I don't know what to say.'

'Don't say anything.' Nick touched her lips with his finger and smiled. A crooked kind of half-smile. 'See you tomorrow, Fi. Sleep well.'

She got out of the car. Walked towards her gate. Stopped and looked back, but it was too dark to see Nick's face so she raised her hand in farewell and carried on.

Nick watched until she was out of sight. Then he started the car and pulled away a little less smoothly than usual.

He should have expected that.

Had she only realised *who* she had been kissing when it had ended?

'Bad luck, Fi,' he heard himself murmur. 'It was only me.'

CHAPTER SEVEN

IT HAD been 'just a kiss'.

So why was it that every time it crept back into Fiona's mind, she felt like something was melting deep inside her body? Making her limbs feel liquid and her brain unable to think of anything other than Nick.

It didn't help that she had every reason to be thinking of Nick the next day when she set out on her shopping expedition. Or that Sam was skipping along beside her, his excitement overflowing.

'It's Uncle Nick's *birthday*! We're going to buy *balloons*!'

Sam helped choose by pointing out the brightest colours he could see for balloons, finding equally festive party hats and several packets of tiny candles. He helped even more by happily disappearing into the toy corner of the bookshop Fiona visited in the hope of finding a perfect gift.

Locating precisely what she was looking for was a thrill. Fiona touch was almost reverent as she turned the glossy pages of the glorious photographic record and beautifully worded descriptions of the settings used for the movie Nick loved. Imagining his pleasure in this gift gave her an anticipation that easily rivalled Sam's level of excitement and there was the added bonus of a personal significance with the inclusion of places she had actually taken Nick to visit in the Glenorchy area.

Had it really been only two weeks ago?

With an effort Fiona closed the book and focused on things that still needed to be done. She moved to another section of the shop to choose wrapping paper and ribbon but her choices were made on autopilot because she was still astonished. She felt much closer to Nick than such a short space of time should have allowed for. Far closer than she had felt when she had first known him. By some magic, in the years apart, things had changed enough to make their connection much stronger.

Paying for her purchases, Fiona wondered what Nick was doing. Finishing a Saturday morning ward round, perhaps? There were always a few geriatric patients that needed ongoing care and there could well be a maternity case or something in the emergency department that needed attention. Being an administrator on top of the hands-on medical duties meant that paperwork inevitably accumulated as well.

But maybe Nick had completed all that needed to be done professionally. He might be home again by now. Out walking the dogs, maybe? Standing on the old jetty and letting the peaceful pull of the mountains and lake nudge him into daydreaming?

Was he thinking about her at all?

About that kiss?

What was it going to be like when she saw him again that evening? It would be impossible not to be watching for some kind of signal. An acknowledgement that something had changed between them. An indication that Nick hadn't been really honest in dismissing what had happened as 'just a kiss'.

Hoping that he hadn't been really honest.

She saw nothing. It was Sam who claimed Nick's attention the instant he stepped through the Murchisons' door later that day.

'We've got balloons, Uncle Nick. And candles…and *cake*!'

'Wow! Is it someone's birthday?'

Sam's grin stretched from ear to ear. 'It's *your* birthday, Uncle Nick. Did you forget?'

'No.' Nick ruffled Sam's hair and then swept him up for a hug. 'I didn't forget. I just wanted to see you smile, buddy.'

It was Elsie who was smiling when her food claimed Nick's attention.

'That was the best roast lamb I've ever tasted, Elsie. You're an amazing cook.'

Elsie blushed modestly. 'I just hope you like chocolate cake.'

The icing on the cake was threatening to melt under the heat of so many candles.

'Sam, I don't think I can blow all these out all by myself.'

Sam made a valiant effort, though it was clearly Nick's breath that extinguished the candles. It created a surprising amount of smoke, which was enough to start Sam coughing, but the short delay to find his inhaler didn't dampen the party atmosphere.

'It's the best cake ever,' Nick decreed.

'I helped,' Sam told him proudly. He was still a little wheezy but he'd stopped coughing. 'And I got to lick the spoon.'

'Lucky you.'

And finally, in the swiftness with which Nick's gaze met hers at the mention of licking something, Fiona saw what she'd been watching for from the moment he had arrived.

The acknowledgement of that kiss.

But it came with a wariness that was crushing.

Things were not going to change between them because Nick did not want things to change.

He *really* didn't want it.

Was she surprised? No. Disappointed? Ridiculously so.

She collected herself, of course. Forced down bites of cake, carefully avoiding eye contact with Nick again. By the time they took their coffee to sit near the fire, when Elsie had shooed them from her kitchen, Fiona was capable of a genuinely happy smile. She was still going to get a lot of pleasure from giving Nick a gift he would appreciate.

Sam sat on the couch beside Nick to help him peel off the wrapping paper.

'*Oh...*' Nick actually seemed lost for words as he gazed as his gift. He opened the cover and seemed to spend a long time staring at the inscription Fiona had written.

To Nick, it said. *On your thirtieth birthday. With my love, Fi*

She'd added a postscript as well.

P.S. Magic happens

Nick had his arm around Sam as he finally looked up at Fiona.

'I love it,' he said simply. 'It's perfect. Thank you so much.'

There was no wariness in his gaze this time. There was something so much softer that Fiona felt her heart squeeze painfully.

With my love, she had written.

She just hadn't realised how much truth those few words held.

She wasn't just attracted to this man.

She was in love with him.

Sam was bemused by the silence around him. 'Show me,' he demanded, snuggling closer to Nick. 'I want to see the pictures, please.'

Fiona sat very still, watching as Nick carefully turned the large pages and Sam leaned in. She heard his eager questions and the rumble of Nick's deep voice as he answered them, but she wasn't listening to what was being said. The sight of the two of them bent over the book, so close to each other, was enough to bring tears to her eyes.

The need to keep Nick in Sam's life—in *her* life—was overwhelmingly powerful. If she was unexpectedly in over her head, it was her problem. She owed it to Sam to find a way to mask her feelings.

If Nick was this wary after that kiss, imagine how fast he would disappear if he had any idea of the truth she had just confronted.

They would never hear from him again. He'd cut himself off once before, hadn't he? The only time Nick had spoken to Al after the wedding had been at the funeral of their parents. If his original family ties hadn't been enough to prevent him vanishing, how could something as new and fragile as what he had found here stand a chance? Maybe there wasn't enough time to strengthen it on this visit but, at the very least, Fiona could try and make sure the idea of a return visit was attractive.

Somehow she had to make Nick feel safe. To reassure him that nothing would change if he didn't want it to.

'Another glass of champagne for anyone?' Elsie came

in with the unfinished bottle Fiona had purchased on the shopping trip she had enjoyed so much that morning, when everything on her list had reminded her of Nick. 'It's a shame to waste it.'

The promise of something more than a birthday to celebrate had already evaporated. Champagne was out of place.

Or maybe not.

With a flash of insight Fiona could see perfectly clearly the path she needed to take right now.

'Not for me,' Fiona said firmly. 'I had enough to drink last night to last me quite a while.' The smile Nick received was apologetic. 'Too much, I suspect, and I'm old enough to know better.'

The message was unmistakable and it felt so like a punch in his midriff that it was actually hard to suck in a new breath.

Fiona was telling him she'd only kissed him because she'd had too much to drink.

But, then, he'd already guessed that she'd imagined herself to be kissing a ghost. Why else would she have said his name with that undertone of appalled realisation?

He could still hear the echo of that whisper.

'Oh, my God…Nick?'

It was a put-down that Nick couldn't shake for the rest of that evening. Especially when things seemed to go from bad to worse. It should have been fun, spending a little time playing cars with Sam before he went to bed, but Fiona had been close by.

'Where's your red and white car, Sam?' she asked brightly. 'Daddy's favourite car was red and white.'

Sam delved into the toy basket. 'Here it is!' He grinned up at Nick. 'I'm going to win now, Uncle Nick. Just like my daddy always did. Did you see him race his red and white car?'

'I sure did, buddy.'

'Did you see him win?'

'Sure.' Somehow Nick found a smile. 'Lots of times.'

Even Elsie was apparently happy to help the slide of Nick's spirits.

'Alistair was a lot older than you, wasn't he, Nick?'

'Ten years.' Would it make any difference to Fiona if she knew how little their relationship had resembled one of brothers? 'He was more like an uncle than a brother.'

'Good grief! That made me like your *aunt*, then?' Fiona's laugh sounded as forced as Nick's smile had been.

'You're *my* uncle,' Sam declared.

No. Nothing was going to help. Nick had been put firmly in his place tonight. The younger brother. The uncle.

No chance of being anything more.

No way of stepping out from the long shadows of the past.

Fiona must have guessed how he felt about her, which was hardly surprising, given that extraordinary kiss. A mistake, from her point of view, and she was now being kind but very carefully building a wall between them.

Brick by brick.

And every one of those damned bricks had his brother's name on it.

It hadn't worked.

The last thing Fiona had wanted was to drive Nick too far away. All she had been trying to let Nick know had been that she was aware of the age gap between them. That she had been his brother's wife and wasn't about to forget how important a role model Al had been for Nick. And that she wouldn't dream of trying to make her relationship with Nick anything other than one of friendship and family.

Instead, she had created a barrier that seemed to be pushing them apart and the distance between them grew over the next few days, as though it had a life of its own.

Not that she had noticed on Monday. It had been so busy that their only interaction had consisted of patient handovers.

'This is Mrs McKay. She's fifty-seven years old and has had an angina attack, which was unresponsive to her GTN. She still has four out of ten chest pain, is tachycardic at 120 and tachypnoea of 30…'

'This is Hayden. He's eight and has a Colles' fracture of his left arm after falling off his bike on the way to school…'

'Siobhan is six months old. Vomiting and diarrhoea since yesterday and she's not feeding well today. Temperature of 38.6…'

'Mr Wright has been short of breath since this morning. He's on home oxygen for COAD, which is currently exacerbated by a chest infection. SP02 is 93 percent on oxygen…'

Things got quieter late in the day but Nick missed his now usual visit to the ambulance station and that was when the first alarm bells rang for Fiona.

She waited for him on Tuesday evening, knowing he was still at work because his little red car was still parked outside. When he didn't appear, she went to his office to find him busy with paperwork.

'Come home for dinner,' she invited. 'Sam's been drawing pictures for you and you know how Mum loves to have her cooking appreciated.'

Nick smiled but he hadn't looked at her for more than an instant and he shook his head.

'I can't keep imposing on you. And…I'm expecting an overseas call. I need to be home tonight.'

On Wednesday afternoon, Fiona had a call to a man with back pain and she called Nick a short time later.

'We're on the way in with a fifty-eight-year-old male with sudden onset "ripping sensation" back and abdominal pain,' she relayed. 'Suspected triple A. Ten out of ten pain, which hasn't responded to 20 milligrams of morphine, and his blood pressure has dropped from 140 over 90 to 110 over 60. I've got two wide-bore IV lines in situ and am running a bolus of saline. GCS has dropped to about 12.'

'You want helicopter evacuation set up?'

'Already organised. Could you meet us over at the helipad? I don't want to take off until he's as stable as possible.'

If her patient had an abdominal aortic aneurysm that was rupturing, there was nothing they could do for him at Lakeview. He needed emergency surgery at a large hospital and even if they got him there, his chances of survival weren't great.

It was no wonder Nick looked grim when he jumped into the back of the ambulance as Shane parked near the helicopter, which was being readied for take-off, its rotors already turning.

'He lost consciousness about two minutes ago,' Fiona said. 'And I can't get a blood pressure…' She looked over her shoulder at the life pack, where the cardiac rhythm on the screen was showing some alarming changes. Shane climbed through from the driver's seat and picked up the bag mask to ventilate their patient.

Nick felt the man's abdomen. 'It's rigid.'

'He's in VF.' The back of the ambulance was the worst of places to try and run a cardiac arrest scenario. Far too cramped. Dangerous, in fact, to defibrillate patients with the metal stretchers and not enough space to get well clear but they had to try.

It was messy. Nick climbed past Fiona to get to the man's head and prepare to intubate him. Fiona delivered a series of shocks that failed to restore a normal heart rhythm and then started chest compressions.

Shane squeezed in to look after bag masking while Nick hung more fluids and used a pressure cuff to try and infuse them rapidly. Then he pulled drugs from Fiona's kit as they continued to fight what they all knew was a losing battle.

When Fiona reached to charge up the machine for the fifth time, she felt Nick's fingers grip her wrist. 'It's time to stop,' he told her gently. 'He's bled out. We've done our best but we can't start a heart that has no blood to work with.'

He was right, of course, but it was never an easy call to accept. Fiona stared at Nick. He looked upset, too, she decided. More than upset. Those shadows under his eyes made it look like he hadn't slept well for days. Fiona wanted to reach out and touch him, to ask if he was OK, but that would be a stupid question at a time like this. None of them were 'OK'.

The silence made her aware of the hiss of oxygen still escaping the main cylinder.

'Is there anything you'd like me to do?' Nick asked. 'What's the protocol?'

'It's a sudden death.' Fiona turned off the oxygen supply. 'We'll have to notify the police and he'll have to be transferred for an autopsy. We'll take him to the morgue for now.' She swallowed. 'His wife was going to follow us in her car. She might be here already.'

'I'll go and talk to her,' Nick offered. 'What's her name?'

'Eileen Wilkins.'

'And *his* name?'

Fiona was removing the ET tube from her patient's mouth. His wife would want to see him and it was important to preserve his dignity for her sake.

'Fi?'

'His name's Alistair.' Fiona was taking out the IV lines now. She didn't look up at Nick. 'His wife called him Al.'

The ambulance rocked as Nick climbed jumped down from the back without saying anything. Had he heard the reluctance in her voice to use that name? Would he understand that she now knew she had been mistaken? Reminding Nick of what he'd lost hadn't been the way to make him feel safe at all. It had had the opposite effect but Fiona had no idea how to fix things. She would have to try, of course, just as she had tried her best for her patient, but she had the horrible feeling that it wasn't going to work.

It was not a good way to finish her day, cleaning up an unsuccessful resuscitation scene. Fiona's spirits lifted a little when she saw Nick coming out of the hospital, heading towards the car park. She abandoned her bucket of hot water and detergent, leaving the mop propped against the back of the ambulance, and headed towards him. Then she noticed his companion and her heart sank.

'Sorry, Jeff. I know I was supposed to ring you but I haven't had a chance yet.'

'Could we talk now? I've got a few ideas about the fundraising campaign.'

Fiona shook her head. 'This really isn't a good time.'

'Yeah. Nick was saying you'd had a bad day. Can I take you out for a drink or something?'

'No.' Fiona shook her head again. 'I'll get back to you next week, OK?'

'I'll call you, shall I?'

Fiona shook her head for the third time, wishing Nick would say something, but he just nodded a farewell as he pulled car keys from his pocket.

'I'll leave you to it,' he said. 'See you tomorrow, Fi.'

She watched him drive away. 'I've got a lot to do,' she said to Jeff. 'Sorry, but I'll have to go, too.'

'Guess I'll get the bus home, then.'

Was he expecting her to offer him a lift? It wasn't the first time this man had made Fiona feel uneasy. Shane's approach was a relief.

'You want me to mop out the truck, Fi?'

'No, I'll do it. See you, Jeff.'

He took the hint but looked less than happy at the blatant dismissal. Shane watched him walk away. 'Funny guy,' he said. 'You sure you want him hanging around?'

'I'm not sure of anything today,' Fiona responded glumly. 'Let's get the truck sorted and go home ourselves.'

'I've tidied the gear. I found this under the stretcher.' Shane reached into his pocket. 'It's yours, isn't it?'

'No.' But Fiona recognised the cellphone. 'It's Nick's. I'll take it and give it back to him tomorrow.'

The phone rang when Fiona was climbing into her car to go home. She flipped it open and answered it, thinking it might be Nick, trying to locate it.

'Nick?' The male voice had an American accent and sounded enthusiastic. 'How are you, buddy?'

'It's not Nick,' she replied. 'He left his phone at work.'

'Damn! I really need to talk to him. I tried his landline number but couldn't get through.'

'Try again. He should be home.'

'I think there's a fault with the line or something. It just beeps. Look, if you see him, can you tell him to ring Doug? I'm with MSF and we've got a job lined up that he's going to love. In El Salvador. We need to get an answer pretty quick, though, 'cos we're finalising the team tonight.'

'I'll pass on the message,' Fiona promised. She could ring him herself, couldn't she?

But what if the landline *was* faulty? Hugh had had problems in the past with lines that went through a stand of old trees before they got to the house on the beach. Maybe Nick was relying on his cellphone and had no idea he'd dropped it during that resuscitation effort. Could it be that worrying about his next job was contributing to how unhappy he'd been looking?

Instead of turning for home, Fiona took the road that led to the Pattersons' property. Returning the cellphone was fate giving her an opportunity she needed. A chance to talk to Nick and let him know how important he was to her family. To *her*. Hopefully, she could do that without stepping over any safe boundaries but if not, well, she would just have to deal with it.

She used her own phone to call her mother. 'I'll be late,' she warned. 'Give Sam a kiss for me but don't hold up dinner.'

'His name was Doug. He said it was important that you call him tonight.'

'It could have waited. You didn't need to come all the way out here, Fi.'

'It's not that far.'

'You probably had better things to do.'

'Like what?' Fiona bent to scratch the ears of the two dogs crowding her at the door. 'Hey, Tuck. Hey, Lass. It's been too long since I've seen you guys.'

'Like going out for a drink with your new admirer.'

'What?' Fiona straightened. 'You mean Jeff? You've got to be kidding! He's not any kind of admirer. He just wants to discuss the fundraising thing.'

Nick turned away. 'Don't be naïve, Fi.'

She followed him. As an opportunity to talk, this was not promising. Nick didn't stop until he reached the kitchen where he was obviously preparing the dogs' dinner. He picked up the knife and continued cutting meat but he gave Fiona a long glance and shook his head as though giving up. 'Why can't you see something for what it really is?'

'I'm not following you.'

'It doesn't matter.'

'I think it does.' Fiona leaned against the bench and watched him cutting the meat. The dogs sat on either side of his legs. They were also watching. The atmosphere was one of expectation but Fiona's wasn't pleasurable. 'What's wrong, Nick?'

'Nothing.'

'I don't believe that. You've been avoiding me in the last few days. You looked miserable today and it wasn't just because we couldn't save a patient.' Fiona's heart was thumping. 'I thought we were friends again, Nick. Talk to me. Please.'

Nick scooped meat into the dogs' bowls. He set them down in a corner of the kitchen near the coal range that was providing the only warmth Fiona could detect here.

'I should ring Doug,' he said finally. 'It's time I sorted out where I'm going next.'

Fiona took a deep breath. She could deal with this. She *had* to.

'You'll come back, though…' It was hard to keep a wobble from her voice. 'Won't you?'

Nick shrugged. 'I'm not sure that would be a good idea.' He opened the fridge and took out a bottle of wine. He held it up and Fiona nodded silently.

Nick poured two glasses of wine and handed one to Fiona. She followed his example and sat down at the table.

'If I'd known I was going to get plunged back into the past, I would never have come,' he said quietly. 'It's not what I wanted, Fi. To tell you the truth, I can't deal with hearing about Al all the time. I stood at his funeral, jammed in behind that media contingent, and I thought at least it was over. I could get on with my life without everything I did—who I *was*—being compared to my brother.'

'Nobody's comparing you. You're totally different people.'

'Not different enough. Same name. Same looks.'

'No. You're different.'

'Not when you've had a glass of wine or two.'

'*What?*' Fiona set her glass down with a bang. She stared at Nick, waiting until he met her gaze.

'Would you have kissed me, Fi? If it hadn't been so easy to imagine you were kissing Al?'

Fiona's mouth had gone dry but there was no way she was picking up that glass of wine again. 'Is that what you thought I was thinking?'

'You can't deny it. You shocked yourself.' Nick's face was expressionless. 'You asked my name as if you couldn't believe you could have made such a mistake.'

'No. You've got it wrong, Nick. It wasn't—'

'And ever since then you've been hauling Al into the conversation whenever you can. So's everybody else. God.' Nick closed his eyes for a second. 'Even your patients are helping to remind me.'

He opened his eyes with a sigh. 'You've got your son growing up to believe his father was a superhero. At least, if I'm not around, he's not going to find out how wrong he is.'

Fiona couldn't believe the words she was hearing. Or the bitter undertone. This was Nick talking. The man she had remembered, until very recently, as a quiet youth who had looked up to his older brother. Had grown up trying, but failing, to live up to standards Alistair had set. OK, he had also lived with the feeling of being invisible in a family where success had meant grabbing headlines but it seemed totally out of character to attack his brother's reputation.

Or had she been protecting that reputation needlessly?

'You sound like you hated him,' she said quietly.

'Let's just say I lost any respect I had for him.'

'When?'

'The night before he married you.'

So she hadn't been wrong about her first impressions. The rift had occurred later—at a time when her life had been changing so much she had barely seen her brother-in-law.

'What happened?'

'It doesn't matter.' Nick drained his glass of wine and began to pour another. 'There's no point in dragging it all out now. You probably wouldn't believe me. And why should you? You had a wonderful marriage. That's all that matters.' Nick took a swallow of the wine. 'I shouldn't have started this conversation.' He gave Fiona a tight smile. 'Just forget I said anything.'

The silence was broken only by the sound of one of the dogs lapping water and then settling back onto the rug by the coal range with a sigh of contentment. Fiona toyed with the stem of her wineglass as the silence continued. If ever there was a time to be honest, this had to be it. She drew in a somewhat shaky breath.

'Actually…it wasn't that wonderful.'

Nick looked up sharply but he said nothing. Just waited.

Fiona sighed. 'Oh, it was to begin with, I guess, but it was never real. I hung on to my job because that *was* real but it meant we had quite long stretches of time apart and when we were together it was one long party. I got to dress up and be with the man every other woman wanted to be with. It wasn't anything like a real marriage.' Fiona had to stop and swallow hard. 'Maybe that's why it took so long to realise I'd made such a mistake.'

Still, Nick said nothing but he was watching her carefully.

'We'd separated, Nick. Nearly a year before he died. It happened slowly. He still stayed in the house every time he was back in London but we had separate rooms. It was only a matter of time before it got out but Al was desperate to avoid the publicity. He always hated anything negative being written about him.'

Nick cleared his throat. 'Why did you separate?'

'It became apparent that some of the rumours weren't just tabloid rubbish. Al was never faithful to me.'

'You *knew* that?'

'Not for a long time. Not for sure. Al was very good at talking his way out of trouble. Using his charm to make sure he got what he wanted. And I suppose I wanted to be wrong.' Fiona held Nick's gaze. 'But that was only part of his life. He *was* a hero to a lot of people. Especially rally racing fans. They didn't need to know the truth. *Sam* doesn't need to know. Is it so wrong to let him be proud of a father he can never even meet?'

But Nick didn't answer the question. He had his own.

'How did you get Sam when you were separated?'

'He was the result of one night. Al was back in the country after a long tour and he was…I don't know… down about something. It was close to the anniversary of your parents' death. He begged me to forgive him. Wanted to try again. Was making all kinds of promises and…I'd been lonely. We had a few drinks…one thing led to another…'

'Did he know you were pregnant?'

'No, but I suggested the possibility, given that we hadn't bothered with protection.'

'And?'

'And that was when I knew there was no possibility of us ever being together again.'

'Why?'

'Because he laughed.'

'He thought the idea of having kids was funny?'

'No. It was a nasty kind of laugh. And he said that if I was pregnant, I'd know what I needed to do about it, wouldn't I?'

'He didn't mean…?' Nick seemed too shocked to finish his question but Fiona nodded anyway.

'Get rid of it? Of course that's what he meant. He didn't want a fat wife. Or a child cramping his lifestyle.'

'My God…' Nick's hand curled into a fist on the tabletop. 'I knew he was a bastard but I had no real idea at all.'

'Why did you think he was a bastard? When I first met you I got the impression you thought he was as wonderful as everybody else thought.'

'I did.'

'Was it at your parents' funeral? When he told you how stupid it would be to waste your medical degree working in Third World countries instead of making a decent living and getting the status of being in private practice?'

'No. Way before that.'

'When?'

'I told you. The night before your wedding. At the stag party. We…had an argument.'

'What about?'

Nick looked away and Fiona touched his hand.

'Please, tell me. I'm not going to be shocked, Nick. Or hurt. I've dealt with all that. I knew exactly what Al was like in the end but I didn't think *you* did. I didn't want to destroy any childhood memories that might be important for you to hang on to. Did he spend the night with another woman, is that it?'

'Yes.'

'And you told him what you thought?'

'More than that. I told him he didn't deserve you.'

The idea of Nick defending her like that gave Fiona that strange melting sensation inside, like remembering his kiss had.

'And?'

'And we had a fight. That black eye wasn't from a patient in Emergency that day, Fi. It had been the punch that finished that fight. The winning blow. Al knocked me out.'

'You were actually *fighting*? For *me*?'

'Yes.'

'Why?'

'Can't you guess?'

Fiona searched Nick's face. He looked so serious. So

sincere. So... She couldn't identify the emotional glue holding everything else together but it made her want to cry.

'I was in love with you, Fi,' Nick said softly. 'Al guessed. He laughed at me.'

'Oh, my God,' Fiona breathed. *'Why?'*

'He said it was a joke. That my only claim to fame was being his brother—the way it had always been. That someone like you would never look at someone like me.'

Fiona touched Nick's face. The tiny scar at the corner of his eyebrow that must be the only physical evidence left of that black eye. 'Your brother was capable of being so charming, Nick,' she said. 'He could also be incredibly cruel.' She traced her finger gently over his cheekbone and down the hollow of his cheek. 'How could I *not* look at someone as amazing as you, Nick Stewart?' She was touching the corner of his mouth now. And smiling. 'Ironic that It's the other way round now, isn't it? I'm so much older. A single mum. Why would someone like you want someone like me?'

'I would.'

Fiona's finger stilled. Her word was just a whisper. 'Why?'

'Can't you guess?' She could feel the crooked smile beneath that fingertip. 'I'm still in love with you, Fi. I've done my best to get past it in the last ten years but I guess I failed.'

Fiona was touching more of Nick's lips now, as though feeling them move might convince her the words were really being uttered.

'Oh-h...I'm glad you failed.' She was still whispering. 'Why?'

'Because...' Her voice became stronger. Surer. 'I'm in love with you, too.'

Nick caught her hand in his. He pressed it against his lips but his eyes never left Fiona's face. She could see a dawning hope but it was mixed with sheer incredulity. Belief in what she was saying had to be the biggest gift she had ever given anybody but it was also the simplest because it was also a gift to herself.

Fiona stood up with her hand still in Nick's and he moved with her. Then Fiona reached up to put her arms around his neck.

'I want you so much,' she said softly. She didn't have to apply any pressure to bring his face close to hers. Close enough to kiss. Her touch was feather soft. Just the briefest taste.

'Make love to me, Nick...'

Had she said the words out loud? She must have. Why else would Nick be sweeping her into his arms like this? Carrying her away from the warmth of the kitchen...

CHAPTER EIGHT

IT SHOULD have been cold down the other end of the house but Fiona felt as if she had flames dancing over her skin.

Nick set her down gently so that she was standing on the floor beside his bed. Big picture windows gave them a background of moonlight reflecting on a lake as black as sin, but the world outside this room may as well have been on a separate planet as far as Fiona was concerned. She focussed instead on the black pools of Nick's eyes, cut off from her line of vision momentarily as she raised her arms to help him pull off the woollen jersey that was part of her winter uniform.

He dropped the garment to the floor and cupped Fiona's neck with one hand as he tilted his head to find her lips. She could have happily lost herself in the gathering intensity of that kiss—the changing pressure of his lips and the incredible excitement the glide of his tongue against hers created—but Fiona was also aware of Nick's other hand moving. The fingers trailed down her neck towards the first button of her shirt and every tiny contact of his skin against hers created such heat the flames kept dancing higher.

Her breasts caught alight at the first touch, seeming to swell into Nick's hand, the nipples chafing against the lace of her bra. Nick's head dropped to place a lingering kiss on the side of her neck and Fiona shivered at the intensity of her pleasure.

'You're not cold, are you?'

'No.' Fiona pressed herself further into Nick's hands. 'Don't stop…'

She could feel his lips curving into a smile against her skin in the hollow between her neck and her shoulder. 'I wasn't planning to,' he murmured, tugging her shirt free from her trousers.

Then Fiona felt the slide of his hands against the bare skin of her back, pausing for just a heartbeat to flick the catch of her bra open. She needed those hands to steady her as Nick kissed her mouth again. No gentle questions were being asked now. Fiona could taste a need as strong as her own. The tie had fallen from her braid and her hair came loose in Nick's fingers, falling around her face. Wild and free—exactly the way Fiona was feeling right now.

She was unaware of moving backwards until she felt the edge of the bed behind her legs and then she was falling, cradled in Nick's arms, still locked into that passionate kiss as they rolled together on the soft surface of the bed covers.

It was taking too long for Nick to undo the buckle of her belt and Fiona's fingers tangled with his as she tried to help. Soft laughter joined the quickened sound of their breathing as she lifted her hips to ease the removal of her last pieces of clothing. Nick leaned over her to open the drawer of the beside cabinet, and the sight of the small package made Fiona catch her breath.

They were really going to do this. To make love. And she had never wanted anything this much in her entire life.

Nick was kneeling on the bed as he leaned over her but

then he sat back on his haunches. His shirt was unbuttoned—had *she* done that? It was still caught in the waistband of his trousers but it was open enough for her to see the skin of his chest, glistening in the moonlight. A smudged V of fine dark hair and nipples that were hard enough to look like pebbles standing on end. Fiona wetted her lips in anticipation and heard Nick catch his breath.

But he didn't move and Fiona suddenly realised she was lying there completely naked while Nick was still mostly clothed. She held her breath, drowning in the gaze she was being subjected to.

'You are *so* beautiful.' His voice was raw with desire. 'I love you, Fi.'

'I love you.' Fiona reached out. She had to touch him. To convince herself that this was really happening. And the new touch of her hands on his bare chest kicked desire to a totally new level.

Her hands dropped to fumble with his belt buckle and the soft sound that came from her throat was one of frustration and unbearable need.

Nick's hands covered hers. Taking over. Managing what she couldn't manage with calm, deft action. And then he was naked, kneeling over her, and it was Fiona's turn to catch her breath again and revel in the beauty of his body. When he moved, it was to draw back the duvet and cover them, but Fiona didn't need the warmth and she couldn't wait.

'Now, Nick,' she whispered. *'Please…'*

And then he was over her. Inside her. The movement so fluid and sure Fiona could only gasp, close her eyes and surrender herself to the power of a passion that built until she knew her world had stopped turning. The spasms of her climax took her somewhere out of any time or place she had ever known.

Nick's cry a few moments later was her name and Fiona held him so hard she was afraid she might be hurting him.

But she was also too afraid to let him go.

That very first kiss had wakened Fiona's senses.

Making love for the first time had taught them there were things she had never experienced before.

Magic things.

The anxiety that had followed that first kiss—waiting to see Nick's acknowledgement and reaction—was not there when Fiona arrived at work the following day. She knew she would see a reflection of exactly what she was feeling herself.

The euphoria of a connection that transcended anything simply physical.

The connection of loving and being loved in return.

There had never been *anything* quite like this.

Fiona's step didn't falter but she could feel time slowing down as she entered the emergency department of Lakeview Hospital that morning with an elderly patient who had slipped on an icy footpath and broken her hip.

The eye contact lasted only for a heartbeat but it was enough to justify her confidence. The bond between herself and Nick was solid.

Growing stronger with every passing minute.

It was going to change every aspect of her life, she realised. Even their professional interaction felt different. More meaningful.

'This is Jessie Barnes,' she told him. 'She's eighty-three and slipped when she was going out to get her newspaper this morning.'

'Darned ice,' Jessie muttered. 'Winter is just the pits, isn't it?'

'It can be,' Nick agreed sympathetically, smiling at his patient.

'Query left neck of femur,' Fiona continued. She knew why Jessie was beaming back at Nick, her pain forgotten for the moment. 'External rotation and shortening. Pain on movement but good response to Entonox and Jessie's been comfortable since we splinted her leg.'

They had used a pillow splint, tying the elderly woman's legs together with the cushioning between them.

'Vital signs?'

Shane rattled off their recordings, which had all been within normal limits.

'Do you keep good health normally, Jessie?'

'Box of birds I am, dear,' she responded. 'Never had a sick day in my life.'

'No previous symptoms,' Fiona added. 'Straightforward slip. Not knocked out but she did get a bit of a bump on the head.'

'Take more than that to knock *me* out,' Jessie said.

'Let's have a look.' Nick bent closer and Fiona watched as he gently palpated the skull beneath wispy, white hair and questioned Jessie further. The calm reassurance he used kept his patient smiling and Fiona found herself also smiling as she pushed the stretcher away.

Had she ever felt *this* good?

Even when she had first been in love with Al?

It was hard to remember. Had it faded so much because it had never been real to begin with? She and Al had come from such different worlds and they had only met because Al had been forced out of his. Threatened by a serious injury and, probably for the first time in his life, feeling vulnerable.

The man she had fallen in love with had been a part of

Alistair Stewart that had had to be buried again as deeply as possible but Fiona had been too blind to see what had been real and what hadn't been. She knew things had gone terribly wrong but had had no idea why.

That wasn't going to happen again.

Nick was a part of her world. Grounded in the same reality. The vulnerability he had might come from the same need to be loved that Alistair had had but there was a huge difference. Al had needed the adoration of the masses. That kind of love from just one person would be enough for Nick. As it was for her.

More than enough—if that person was Nick.

It was just so perfect. Impossible to hide. And the staff of Lakeview guessed very quickly.

'You…and Nick?' Megan asked on her second visit to the hospital that day. 'Is there something going on here?'

Fiona had done nothing more than smile but Megan had sighed enviously and then grinned. 'You lucky thing. Wow! Wait until I tell Lizzie she was right!'

Shane also noticed. 'Couldn't have happened to a nicer person,' he said. 'Good to know that Nick will be hanging around for a while.'

Would he? Fiona's smile faltered for an instant. They needed to talk about the future but it was too soon, wasn't it? Then again, the luxury of time was something they didn't have. Hugh and Maggie were due back next week. Nick still had to return that call to Doug. They *had* to talk about the future. Their future. Before it was too late.

Even Sam noticed the change in the atmosphere around him that evening when Nick was visiting, although he had no idea what was causing it.

'You look different, Mummy,' he said as he received his goodnight kiss.

'Do I, sweetheart? I'm just the same me.'

'No.' Sam's eyes were drifting shut already. 'You look all…shiny.'

'Shiny, huh? I like that.' The length and passion of Nick's kiss was more than satisfactory. 'I think I'm feeling shiny, too.'

Fiona snuggled closer on the couch near the glow of the fire. 'Mmm.' She wanted another kiss but she knew where that would lead and making love to Nick in her own house—with Sam asleep in the next room—didn't feel quite right. Yet. Besides, there was no telling how early her mother would get home from the restaurant Bernie had taken her to for dinner. 'Shiny's good,' she added.

'Let's keep it like this,' Nick said quietly. 'For ever.'

Fiona's heart skipped a beat. For ever was the biggest commitment. One that she couldn't make until she was sure it was safe. For Sam as much as for herself.

'You and me and Sam,' Nick continued. 'Here…'

Fiona felt her heart thump again. Did that make all this just a fantasy? Nick was no stranger to the lure of magic but if being here was an escape from reality, it was not a world she could share.

'Would you be happy here?' she asked. 'What about your job?'

'I think it's time for a change of direction. I'll have to go away for some training, I guess, but I want to come back. This feels like home. If I had a place like Hugh's— where I could see the lake and the mountains—maybe with a bit of land, I would never want to live anywhere else.'

Fiona ignored the tiny doubts trying to edge into her mind. She went even further and stamped on them firmly. Took another step towards commitment.

'I have a bit of land,' Fiona told Nick. 'Quite a lot, actually. It's on the other side of the lake towards Glenorchy. You know, where we went to that forest?'

'How could I forget? That was the day I knew magic really existed. The day I knew how much in love with you I still was. Always will be…'

Another kiss. A long snatch of time being held in each other's arms. Touching. *Loving*. Ignoring the fact that Nick had used the word 'magic' yet again.

'I bought the farm years ago with the idea of building a house there one day,' Fiona said eventually. 'But we've been so happy here with Mum that it's just been left on the back burner.'

'Your mum was looking pretty happy herself tonight. Do you think there's something going on with her and this Bernie?'

'I hope so.' Fiona smiled. 'I want everybody I love to be as happy as I am.'

'It all sounds perfect,' Nick decided after another kiss.

'Doesn't it? With a new ambulance station and upgraded surgical facilities, Lakeview will take off. We'll both be able to do exactly what we want with the rest of our lives.'

'Sounds like a lot of fundraising coming up.'

'Not necessarily.' Fiona chewed her bottom lip. 'I've kept it really quiet for obvious reasons but you must realise I've got far more money than I could ever use, thanks to my inheritance from Al. There's a trust fund for Sam but that barely dented it. Hugh's one of the trustees for another trust I set up so he's one of the few people that know it was me that paid for most of our new helicopter last year. We could still do a lot with the rest and there would be enough community support to disguise where the extra money was coming from.'

They were still talking—between kisses—exploring the possibilities their futures could hold, when Elsie finally got home, well after midnight. Fiona and Nick scrambled up from the couch but still needed to stand close enough to be touching.

'Look at the time!' Fiona exclaimed. 'You're very late, Mum.' Then she stared at her mother and her lips curved into a smile. 'I know exactly what Sam meant now.'

Elsie peeled off her coat and gloves. 'I *am* old enough to stay out as late as I feel like, you know.' She was looking from Fiona to Nick and back again.

'You look shiny, Mum.'

'I…um…' Elsie was looking bemused. 'What's going on, Fi? You…and Nick?'

'Yeah…' Fiona couldn't stop smiling. 'I was about to ask you the same thing. You…and Bernie?'

'Yeah…' Elsie was smiling back at her daughter and Nick was smiling at both of them.

'Wonderful, isn't it?' he said. 'Being shiny?'

Fiona and Elsie answered in unison. 'Yeah…'

On Saturday, despite the freezing weather with the first flurries of winter snow, Fiona took Nick to see the stretch of land she owned.

'It's not a small farm. There's a line of trees on that hill over there that marks one boundary and it goes as far as the river on the other side and all the way down to the lake here.'

'How on earth do you manage it?'

'I don't. I've got a farm manager who lives in a house up near those trees.'

'I hope he appreciates the view.'

'Do you like it, Nick?'

'I love it. I think I prefer this side of the lake. I like

seeing the Remarkables from a distance instead of having them glowering over my shoulder.'

'There's any number of great building sites. We've got some small patches of forest as well. *We* love it, don't we, Sam?'

'We can go bear hunting, Uncle Nick.'

'Absolutely. Would you like to live here, Sam?'

'No.'

'Why not?'

'It would be too cold,' Sam said patiently. 'It's snowing and there's no house for us.'

Fiona laughed as she stood there with Nick's arms and body shielding her from the icy wind, watching her little boy running around with his mouth open and tongue out, trying to catch snowflakes.

Was it too soon to feel this happy? This secure?

It had only been days since they had discovered their love. Since that first kiss. Since Nick had needed reassurance that it was him she was in love with and that she wasn't chasing Al's ghost. Was she being naïve yet again in thinking they had overcome any obstacles?

She turned her face up to smile at Nick and felt the brush of snowflakes on her cheeks.

'Do you remember…?' she began, but then she trapped her next words by biting her lip.

What had Nick said the other night? That he couldn't deal with hearing about Al all the time? This memory came from a time that had included Al so maybe she shouldn't bring it up. It might spoil an otherwise perfect moment.

Would she always have to be careful what she said? Would the easy way in which Sam's father was often spoken of become awkward? A no-go area even?

That would confuse Sam and if Fiona tried to explain, it might affect his relationship with Nick.

Lord, it was a potential minefield.

'Do I remember what?' Nick prompted.

'That day we made the snowman.'

'I've never forgotten a minute of it. You were not only the most gorgeous woman I'd ever seen but you really knew how to play.' His voice dropped. 'You were just perfect, Fi.' He hugged her closer and Fiona let herself relax. She pushed those niggling doubts into submission. 'You still are.' With a glance to check that Sam was still busy on his own mission, he nuzzled Fiona's neck. 'Play with me tonight?'

The shiver of anticipation was, quite simply, delicious.

'If Mum's going to be home to babysit,' Fiona murmured, 'just try and stop me.'

'If this weather keeps up, we might get snowed in for days.'

Fiona laughed again. 'Even better!'

They didn't get snowed in but it was bitterly cold on Sunday morning. Fiona had no intention of getting out of bed in any hurry.

Not when she was sharing this warmth with Nick.

And not when she was tired from lack of rest but so contented she felt like sufficient sleep was something she could happily forgo for the rest of her life.

'Where did you learn to make love like that, Nicholas Stewart?'

'It's not me, it's you.' Nick's hand traced the mound of Fiona's shoulder and trailed down to skim her breast. 'I've never experienced anything like last night before.'

'Me neither.'

The raised eyebrow was a question. Did Nick really want to know how he compared with any past lovers? To his brother? Fiona wasn't going to step anywhere near that minefield and there was no reason to. This was about Nick. No one else. But didn't every man want reassurance that his love-making was the best? There was only one thing that really made the biggest difference.

'I don't think it's me *or* you,' she told him softly. 'It's the combination and the way we feel about each other. We're perfect together, that's all.' So perfect it was almost too much to bear and so Fiona smiled. 'In spite of me being an older woman.'

'You know that's never mattered a damn to me. Does it really bother you?'

'Not any more. And the older we get, the less it'll matter. By the time you're fifty you'll probably look ten years older than me.'

Nick lay back with a groan. 'I *feel* ten years older this morning. Are you going to keep me up all night, every night?'

'Yep.' Fiona was unrepentant. 'And seeing as it's Sunday today, I might just keep you in bed till lunchtime.'

'But it's a day of rest.'

'You can rest later.' Fiona inched closer so that every possible patch of her skin was in contact with Nick's.

The ringing of the phone on the bedside table was a very unwelcome intrusion.

'You're not on call, are you, Nick?'

'No.'

'Don't answer it, then.'

'But it might be for you.'

'I'm not on call either.' But she did have other responsibilities, didn't she?

Like her son.

Nick picked up the phone. 'Elsie,' he said a moment later. 'Is something wrong?'

Fiona snatched the phone from his hand. 'Mum? What's happened? Is Sam all right?'

'He's fine.'

'Are *you* all right?' Stupid question. She could tell from her mother's voice that she was far from all right.

'You won't have seen the papers yet. Bernie's here— he brought a copy with him.'

'What's happened? Who's hurt? My God, something hasn't happened to Hugh and Maggie, has it?'

'No.' Her mother was silent for a moment. 'I can't tell you over the phone, darling. I think it's something you need to see for yourself. I'm sorry, but you'd better come home.'

CHAPTER NINE

THE telephone was ringing.

Again.

Bernie picked it up. 'No,' he said brusquely. 'She has no comment to make.'

'Turn it off,' Elsie begged. She turned back to where Fiona and Nick sat at the dining-room table in the Murchison house, the pages of a national Sunday newspaper spread before them, an anxious frown creasing her face as she looked at her daughter. 'You're awfully pale, darling. Are you all right? Can I get you anything?'

Fiona shook her head in answer to both queries. Nothing was going to make this all right. Her world was in the process of crashing down around her.

'I just don't understand,' she said, not for the first time. 'How could this have happened? We've been so careful!'

'Someone's put two and two together,' Bernie said heavily.

'But how?' Fiona cast a worried glance at Sam but he was busy, happily joining cardboard tubes into a long tunnel. Her son was blissfully unaware that his world was threatened. Fiona blinked back tears and her sad query was almost inaudible. 'And *why*?'

'That's pretty obvious from the point of view of an outsider,' Bernie said.

Fiona raised her eyebrows. This may not be the best way to meet the man who had captured her mother's heart but right from the first handshake and sympathetic smile she had liked this man. He had the air of an intelligent person who had seen a great deal in his life but had retained compassion and tolerance.

Right now he was holding both his hands up in a gesture of resigned acceptance. 'It's a great story,' he said frankly. 'The brother of a world-famous driver at the scene of an accident rather similar to the one that killed his only sibling. Added bonus—the son of the famous driver has been living secretly under a different name in a small New Zealand town. His mother—who could still be living the life of the rich and famous—is a local heroine, responsible for saving lives.' Bernie gave an incredulous huff. 'I have to say *I* was blown away by it all.'

'But how did they find out? *Where* did they get all these photos?'

'That one of you was in the local papers last year,' Elsie reminded her. 'When the new helicopter arrived, remember?'

'It's a pretty old one of me,' Nick said. 'I think it was part of a *National Geographic* article on MSF.'

And the one of Alistair was the same one that took pride of place on the Murchisons' mantelpiece. So familiar—but never seen printed right beside a picture of Nick.

'I hadn't noticed how like Al you look,' Elsie murmured. 'Maybe someone saw you and thought you *were* Alistair.'

Fiona said nothing. She'd *been* that someone, for just a heartbeat.

'They've certainly taken that line.' Bernie's snort was contemptuous. 'How sensationalist can you get?' He read aloud from the article in the lifestyle section of the popular weekend newspaper. '"Forget Elvis. There's another king living the life of a recluse right here in New Zealand. Still alive? Almost. From the ashes of well-documented family tragedy, the Stewart clan is reborn…"'

Bernie's voice trailed away. They had all read the words. Nobody wanted to hear them again. Fiona didn't dare look at Nick. She could just imagine how tightly bunched the muscles of his jaw would be. This was more than undoing any reassurance she had tried to give him—that she had known she had been kissing him and not some ghost.

'Someone's certainly done a bit of homework,' Bernie said into the silence. 'But I don't think it would have been that difficult. Not with the kind of resources the internet can provide.' He leaned over the newspaper again. 'The name of that reporter doesn't ring any bells for anyone? Trevor Hayes?'

'No.' Fiona leaned on her elbows, her forehead against her palms. 'I don't know any reporters except that local guy that did the stuff on the helicopter campaign. I certainly haven't spoken to anyone recently.'

'The campaign,' Nick said slowly. Then he snapped his fingers. 'Of course. *Jeff.*'

He had Bernie's full attention instantly. 'Who's Jeff?'

'He's a freelance journalist. Got injured in the rally race incident and Fi's kind of taken him under her wing since then. He's supposed to be helping write publicity material for the new fundraising campaign coming up.'

'He doesn't know about my private life,' Fiona said. She had made sure of that quite deliberately. 'And he's never met Sam.'

'He saw his photo, though, didn't he? On your desk.'

'Oh, my God,' Fiona breathed. She was staring back at Nick, a cold trickle of fear running down her spine. 'And you...*you* said he was your nephew.'

Nick held her gaze but his expression became curiously bland. Did she think she was blaming him for this?

Maybe she was, indirectly. He was the only person who had the surname that could have led to a successful internet search for someone who was curious. Or maybe someone who had known what they had been looking for. How long had Jeff been interested in the rally car scene? Who had *he* been talking to?

'What name does Sam have on his birth certificate?' Bernie asked.

'Murchison-Stewart,' Fiona replied. 'But he's only registered as Murchison at his kindergarten.'

'That's what I really don't like.' Elsie set a teapot down on the table. 'The idea that they were at Sam's kindy, taking photos, and we didn't know anything about it. What were they *thinking*?'

'I think I'll look into that,' said Bernie.

Fiona turned again to look at her son. Sam had propped one end of his long tunnel up on cushions and was poking his small cars into the hole. They came shooting out the other end. Sam looked up and grinned. 'Did you see that, Uncle Nick? Did you see how *fast* it went?'

'Sure did, buddy.'

'I'll do it again,' Sam said. 'Watch!'

Fiona watched as well but she couldn't share Sam's enjoyment. The picture in the newspaper had been of Sam playing with cars. Not that it would have been hard to stage and it couldn't have been a better shot for the angle the article had taken. A child who had car racing in his blood, being hidden away and denied a world he could have been part of. A world that would be many a small boy's dream.

Was she really a villain, trying to give him an ordinary life?

Bernie was watching Sam as well and Fiona didn't like the concern she could see on the retired detective's face.

'This guy's got a hell of a nerve,' Nick was saying. 'Fancy suggesting that a fundraising campaign for the ambulance service is hardly necessary, given the kind of wealth you must have tucked away.'

'Are they exaggerating?' Bernie asked quietly.

Fiona shrugged, swallowing a new prickle of fear. 'They're not far off the truth.' And the children of very wealthy people could be a target for such horrors as kidnapping, couldn't they?

Elsie saw the look that passed between Bernie and Fiona and the tea she was pouring wobbled and slopped onto the tabletop. She picked up a serviette and mopped at the puddle.

'Oh, my…' she worried aloud. 'I hadn't thought of anything like that. What will we do? Keep Sam at home?'

'No!' Fiona didn't mean to sound so fierce but she had worked too hard to create this life for herself and her family. She wasn't going to let it be ruined.

The possibility of this happening had occurred to her, hadn't it? Back when she had first seen Nick at the disaster scene that day. When she had just crossed her fingers that nobody would make the connection.

How naïve. It had only been a matter of time. What on earth made her think it would be possible to have a relationship with Alistair's brother and not step back into a world she had been so determined to leave behind?

And what would the papers make of *that* when it became known, as it inevitably would? She'd be more than an over-protective mother then. Keeping it all in the family, the headline would probably suggest. Who better to replace a dead hero husband than the spare younger brother?

Nick would find that as intolerable as she would.

It could never work.

The domino effect was making her head spin but it really didn't matter what the fallout was for *her*, did it? She'd been through worse. The only thing that really mattered was Sam and his safety. Emotional as well as physical.

The sound of a cellphone ringing made them all jump.

'It's mine,' Nick said. 'Excuse me.' He got up from the table as he answered the call, walking away to converse with someone. He smiled at Sam—still sending cars down the cardboard tunnel—as he went past. On his way back he paused to click the wheels back onto the faulty blue car.

'It'll go faster now.' He moved towards Fiona but stopped a pace or two away.

A safe distance?

'There's a woman I really should see at the hospital,' he said apologetically. 'One of our geriatric patients who sounds like she's running into a bit of heart failure.' His smile was grim. 'And Lizzie tells me there's a couple of reporters hanging around. What do you want me to say to them?'

Too much had already been said. 'Nothing,' Fiona snapped.

'Maybe I could take the spotlight away from you,' Nick said quietly. 'And from Sam.'

'Not a bad idea,' Bernie said.

'It's my fault they've made the connection,' Nick continued. 'So I'd like to try and repair the damage. I could give them an interview. Tell them what it was like to come face to face with my personal ghosts at that disaster and deal with them.'

She'd been a personal ghost, hadn't she? Fiona clung to Nick's gaze. Had he 'dealt' with her? What the hell was he intending to tell the media about that?

'You'd only encourage them,' she said. 'They'll be hounding you. You won't be able to go anywhere without people pointing you out as Alistair Stewart's brother.'

'So what's new?' Nick's smile was devoid of any amusement. 'I was dreaming to think I could escape my past, Fi. It could never work.'

Did he mean getting away from being overshadowed by his older brother?

Or was he echoing her grim fear for the future of any relationship between them?

'You'd better do what you think is best, then,' she said tightly. 'You've probably had more practice in dealing with reporters than any of us. You grew up with them after all.'

Maybe he would even enjoy the attention—the way every other member of his family always had. No, enjoyment wasn't quite the right word for their attitude to the media. It had been more like a need. A kind of addiction. As though they hadn't existed unless other people had noticed. This was bringing back all sorts of unpleasant memories for Fiona. Addictions could be hereditary. Maybe this was the start of Nick's turn to be famous.

'I'm not without a bit of experience myself,' Bernie said. 'I'll deal with anyone who comes here today.'

Nick nodded. 'And maybe it's better if I don't come back here today.'

Fiona had to look away from Nick's steady gaze. He wanted her to contradict the suggestion but right now

Fiona just wanted to gather her family around her and lock the doors.

To try and turn the clock back and make her life as safe as it had been.

Before Nick had come here.

'Mummy! My tunnel's broken!'

'Is it, sweetheart? Let me see.' The move to help Sam was automatic. It was also a perfect delaying tactic so Fiona could decide the best way to handle this situation. For her own sake, she wanted to have Nick close. He, of all people, should be able to understand why she had to fight any pull back to Al's world. But for her family…? It had been Nick's presence that had started this. The closer he was, the more interest would be taken. Especially in Sam. The new generation. The Stewart the world hadn't known about.

The decision was made by not being made. By the time Fiona walked towards Sam and then looked back, Nick was gone.

CHAPTER TEN

IT WAS late afternoon by the time Nick folded his long frame into the driver's seat of his car and headed home.

Back to Hugh's house.

He couldn't go back to the Murchisons'. Not when Fiona's silence had been acquiescence to his offer to stay away.

It had stopped raining but the roads were wet. It wasn't until he almost lost traction on a corner that Nick realised the speed he was travelling at and he groaned aloud as he slowed the vehicle. What the hell was he doing?

Trying to become his brother?

He'd stopped doing that at ten years old. When he'd realised that he didn't stand a chance of winning the kind of unconditional love his parents had lavished on Al.

When he'd escaped into the fantasy that books could provide—at least until he'd found a new outlet in academia. He'd excelled in medical school but that had been enough to impress his adventurous parents and brother, had it? None of them had attended his graduation. They'd all been too busy, away competing in their chosen sports.

Dammit! He hadn't thought this much about the past in years. Wouldn't have believed it was possible to still feel that old resentment. It felt like he was travelling backwards, dismantling the life he had built. Maybe that was because it had been built on shaky foundations.

Had joining MSF really been the way to distance himself from his brother's orbit after he'd married Fiona or had he, on some level, still been trying to win approval by following in Al's footsteps? Taking the most adventurous path a career in medicine could provide?

Was he still doing that now, dreaming of a future with Fiona as *his* wife? With him being a real father figure to Sam?

No!

His love for Fiona was real. It always had been.

Nobody else would see it that way, though, would they?

Did it matter?

Hell, yes!

He had to know that Fiona's love was as genuine as his own. It wouldn't be good enough to be getting what he dreamed of simply because he was stepping into shoes that could no longer be filled by their owner.

He was a different person from his brother. A very different person.

And, dammit… He was *proud* of who he was.

He pulled off the road onto a deserted lookout area. He slammed the door shut as he got out and he stood with his back to the lake, oblivious to the bite of the freezing wind buffeting him, staring at the shrouded peaks of the Remarkables.

OK, he wasn't as famous and rich as Al had been but he had qualities Al had never had.

He was capable of commitment to a single person. For better or worse. He had an inner strength that meant he could survive anything the rest of the world chose to throw at him. He could take what life offered and make the best of it with good grace. He didn't have to get exactly what he wanted because he'd grown up learning how to deal with not getting it.

But if *he* wasn't *exactly* what Fiona wanted—the part of him that was nothing like his brother—then he would move on.

Because love was the only thing he couldn't compromise on and take what was offered and make the best of it. Making the best of what Fiona offered—if it wasn't just for him—could never work. Not long term. It would destroy him. Tear him apart, piece by little piece.

Even if Fiona was prepared to try and forget Alistair and never compare him to his brother, the rest of the world would do it for her. Her son might do it. Sam was already proud of who his father had been. Nick could imagine a teenage version of Sam confronting him over some issue.

'You're not my real father,' he might say, *'and you never will be, no matter how hard you try.'*

Nick finally shivered and realised how cold he was becoming and how tightly his fists were clenched. It was hard to flex his fingers enough to open the car door again. He paused for another moment before climbing into shelter, however, taking one more glance at those rugged peaks behind him. The clouds were thicker now, getting ready to dump large amounts of snow.

He could deal with this. He could stand beside Fiona and weather any storm. Protect her and Sam. It was what he wanted to do more than he'd ever wanted anything. Even a childhood trying to win the approval and love of his family faded into insignificance compared to this desire.

He was here and if Fiona could show him that she needed him—for himself—then he would never want to be anywhere else.

* * *

Nick hadn't come back.

Bernie went home, finally confident that nobody was going to come knocking on the Murchisons' door.

'It'll be yesterday's news by tomorrow,' he told Fiona. 'It's not as though you're a stranger here. Your mother is well respected in all sorts of community groups and a lot of people think the world of her.' His look suggested that he himself was now Elsie's number-one fan. 'And of you, too, Fiona. Look at how many people have called or texted you this afternoon, offering support.'

This was true. So many people *had* called her mobile.

But not Nick. And that hurt.

'I'm going to visit Sam's kindy tomorrow,' Bernie said in parting. 'They could do with a few hints on security, I think. That is, if you don't mind.'

'I'd appreciate that,' Fiona said.

The evening ritual was the same as always. Dinner and a bath for Sam. Stories and bedtime.

The ordinary was all the more precious because it was under threat but, oddly, it felt incomplete. To everybody.

'Where's Uncle Nick?' Sam asked.

'He's busy, sweetheart.'

'But I want him to tell me a story.'

'Maybe next time.'

'When's next time?'

'I don't know.' Maybe there wouldn't *be* a next time.

'Why doesn't Uncle Nick come and live with us, Mummy? Then he could tell me stories every night. And play cars with me…and…and…' Sam's eyes widened with the excitement of his new idea. 'And it would be like having a daddy, wouldn't it?'

Fiona kissed her son, rubbing her nose gently in his hair.

He still smelled of baby sometimes. Soft and warm and vulnerable.

'Snuggle down,' she whispered with a catch in her voice. 'It's time to go to go to sleep, my love.' Fiona kissed her fingertip and then touched the tip of Sam's nose. 'Sweet dreams.'

She dimmed the light and took a final look at her son before leaving his bedroom, her heart heavy.

Nick had said he'd been dreaming. That it could never work. She wasn't going to be the only person hurt if he chose to leave and the thought of Sam's bewilderment or pain was enough to stir a new emotion into today's mix of disappointment and fear.

Anger.

Who did Nick Stewart think he was, swanning into their lives like this? Giving them all the opportunity to fall in love with him? And then just deciding it wasn't going to work and leaving again—which was what his silence for the rest of today was suggesting.

'Fi?' Her mother was calling from the sitting room. 'Come here, darling. Quickly!'

'What is it?'

'Local news on television. I just switched over and they're interviewing Nick.'

And so they were. He was standing outside Lakeview Hospital, looking so serious and impossibly gorgeous with his dark eyes, the equally dark shadow of his jaw and his hair tousled by the wind.

'...are both New Zealanders. This is their home and they have the right to live their lives here without having their privacy invaded.'

'He just said it was coincidence that brought him here,'

Elsie said breathlessly, 'and that finding he has family was a miracle after the tragedies of his past.'

Fiona had missed the next question being asked by the female reporter.

'…whatever it takes to protect them,' Nick was saying calmly. 'And if that means taking myself and my connections back to some obscure Third World country, then, yes, that's exactly what I'll do.'

Fiona gasped.

'He doesn't mean that,' Elsie said quickly. 'Or, if he does, maybe he's just thinking short term. Going away for a bit to let the fuss die down.'

Fiona said nothing. If Nick went away, he would never come back. You wouldn't go through the pain of breaking a relationship and then front up for potentially more of the same further down the track.

But it was what she wanted, wasn't it? To have her life back the way it had been?

She wanted safety for Sam. It wasn't so much the dramatic and unlikely event of someone kidnapping her son. It was more that public interest would be awakened. His life would be held up for public scrutiny. He might end up thinking—like Al had done—that what other people thought of you was more important that what you thought of yourself.

Obscurity had been a goal in setting up this life but that was already lost.

And if Nick went away, he would be taking too much with him.

Too much of her heart.

She would never feel whole again.

The interview was over and a local weather forecaster was discussing the possibility of heavy snow over the next couple of days. The ski season could kick off nice and early this year.

Elsie switched off the television. 'Don't let him run away,' she said quietly. 'It's not the answer for any of you. He said he wanted to protect you and he can't do that unless he's prepared to stay.'

Fiona picked up the phone. She rang the Patterson house but the line was engaged.

She tried Nick's cellphone but it went straight to voice-mail.

'Leave a message,' Nick's voice told her. 'I'll get back to you just as soon as I can.'

A message? Saying what?

I love you, Nick, but I'm scared. I ran away from my past because I was so hurt by it all. I don't want to get hurt again. I really don't want Sam to get hurt…

No. It wasn't something she could leave in a message. She needed to be with Nick to talk to him. To read his body language. To touch…and be touched when words were not enough.

Maybe Nick was scared as well. There had been some-thing about him in that interview. The way he had held himself so still. The way his careful words had revealed nothing too personal. He hadn't been enjoying the atten-tion at all. He was hiding from the world. Perhaps he was hiding from her, too and that was why he hadn't come back or even rung.

He was keeping himself 'invisible'. Protected.

And why would you do that if you weren't afraid of being hurt?

If nothing else, Fiona could reassure Nick that he was loved. For himself. That she understood.

She tried to call him again but the line was still busy.

* * *

The phone call had been unexpected.

Unnerving.

'How the hell did you get this number?'

'I have my sources.'

'What did you say your name was?'

'Trevor Hayes. Recognise it, mate?'

'You wrote the article in today's paper.'

'Yeah…' The drawl was smug. 'Nice, huh? Or didn't you think so?'

'I think it's bloody lucky you're on the other end of a phone line. *Mate.*'

The laughter was a warning. 'I'm just hitting my stride, Dr Stewart. Wait till you see the next instalment.'

Nick wanted to hang up. His finger hovered over the cut-off button on the phone but something held him back. This man was an enemy. Nick needed to know who and what he was going to fight.

'Amazing what you can find on the internet,' the unpleasantly confident voice continued. 'Bit of a player, your brother, wasn't he?'

'Tabloid papers thrive on the kind of rubbish so-called reporters find when they don't give a damn about the truth.'

Trevor chuckled, unfazed. 'He was the famous one in the family, wasn't he? Did you get a bit jealous?'

'No.'

'Fancied the same things, maybe? Like his *wife*?'

Nick recognised the prickle on the back of his neck. He got it in war zones when things were about to hit the fan. This man was dangerous. He had the power to *really* hurt Fiona.

'Or did you share?' The softness of the words only accentuated their venom. 'Like nice brothers might?'

Nick remained silent. Was this call being recorded?

'How long's the affair been going on, mate? Is that little guy really your nephew? Looks rather like a chip off the old block to me. *Your* block, that is.'

'You could get sued for printing something like that. You *will* get sued, believe me.'

'Who said I'm going to print it? A picture tells a thousand words, mate. From what I've heard it's only a matter of time until we get a great shot of you and your sister-in-law. Nothing to stop me digging up some old stories. Punters are smart. They can read between the lines.'

'You won't get away with it.'

Nick hadn't felt this angry since…since that night in the washroom, facing Alistair and trying to stand up for Fiona.

'Be fun trying. Hey, I caught that interview you did for Lakeside TV. You could be right, you know.'

'What about?'

'Scarper off to the other side of the world and there won't be much point to my story, will there? Why don't you push off back to where you came from?'

'Are you trying to *blackmail* me?'

'Ooh! Nasty word. No. I've got this bet with a mate, see? Told him I could get you off the scene.'

'And why would you want to do that?'

As if he couldn't guess. Trevor had to be a mate of Jeff's. Jeff wanted a clear field to see if he had a chance with Fiona.

The mocking laughter over the telephone line was eerily reminiscent of the way Al had laughed at him so long ago.

'Let's just call it "brotherly love", eh? Hey! Isn't that an awesome headline for the next instalment?'

* * *

The phone rang again a short time later.

Nick was still pacing, furious at how powerless he felt. He could no more fight the pain this journalist was capable of inflicting than he could fight his brother's ghost.

Memories. Innuendo. Intangible things that shouldn't be such a threat but they were. And they were capable of hurting the only people Nick truly loved.

Fiona. And, worse…Sam. Fiona had been right. There was absolutely no point in destroying a little boy's pride in who his father had been. If this Trevor got away with anything in print, it would come back to haunt Sam. Someone would remember. He would get taunted at school. He would learn to make at least part of himself invisible.

Nick snatched up the phone, thinking it was Trevor again. Ready to start doing battle.

But it was Doug. One of the medics lined up for the new project had pulled out. They needed Nick for at least a three-month posting. How soon could he leave?

The timing of this call was fate stepping in. Trevor could win his bet. There would be no story if he wasn't here. Not that Jeff stood a chance but, as much as Nick hated the idea, this was the only way he could protect Fiona.

A call to Hugh cleared the way to leave Lakeview Hospital with GP cover for just a few days. The internet search for suitable flights took the longest time, especially when some glitch in the phone line temporarily disconnected him.

By the time Nick picked up his mobile phone and saw the call he had missed from Fiona, it was nearly 2 a.m. Far too late to call her back. His flight out of Queenstown wasn't due to leave until late afternoon tomorrow, however. That should leave more than enough time to go through a farewell process that could only be painful.

Short-term pain. Better than trying to fight the intangible.

You couldn't live in the past.

Or even *with* the past in this particular instance. Fiona didn't want that any more than he did, and there was no way any of them could escape if they were together because the past was the *reason* they were together.

There simply wasn't a way to remove that part of the equation and see if there was enough left to build a future on.

Their love was too new. Too fragile to withstand the threat that Trevor represented.

Too precious to stay around and participate in its destruction.

Nick had seen that moment of indecision in Fiona's eyes when he'd suggested it was better if he didn't return to the Murchison house that afternoon. And something else. Not blame exactly but recognition that this wouldn't be happening if he wasn't here. Something more like… regret.

That had hurt as much as blame. And Fiona didn't know the half of it, did she?

But maybe if he left now, before any more damage could be done, Jeff and his mate would lose interest. Given time, there might be a chance to come back.

To try again.

CHAPTER ELEVEN

THE silence was eerie.

Even though it was still dark as Fiona dressed the next morning, grateful to end a sleepless night, she knew it had been snowing heavily. She could feel that peculiar, muffled quality of the world outside her window.

There was nothing muffled about the acoustics inside the house, however.

'Mummy! It's *snowed*!' Sam was shrieking with excitement. 'I want to make a snowman.'

'We'd better get you out of your pyjamas, then. Let's take your clothes in by the fire and you can get dressed where it's nice and warm.'

'Ga! I'm going to make a *snowman*!'

'Not until you've got something hot in your tummy, young man. Come and have your porridge.'

Fiona rubbed the condensation from a window and looked out on a white-shrouded garden. 'I'll have to put chains on the car. The ploughs won't get this far up the hill for a while. No kindy for you today, Sam.'

'Do you need to go into work so early?' Elsie set a bowl of hot cereal in front of Sam. 'You won't get off the main roads with an ambulance.'

'We've got the Jeep. And the chopper. We'll only be going out for real emergencies today but I still need to be on station.'

Not just for work. Fiona needed to see Nick. To talk to him. She had done a lot of thinking in those sleepless hours when the snow had been falling. Thoughts that could only be shared with one person.

But his car was not in the car park when she arrived at Lakeview Hospital. It still wasn't there an hour later when Fiona had checked the supplies in the Jeep and had been in contact with the police and fire service to discuss access issues for emergency calls today.

She walked over to the hospital.

'He's stuck,' Lizzie told her. 'Snowed in.'

If only it had happened yesterday. They could have been cut off from the outside world and reality wouldn't have intruded. Fiona could have had another whole day of the bliss she had discovered in Nick's arms. Fantasy, yes, but irresistible nonetheless.

'We've got GP cover,' Lizzie continued. 'Apparently it's been organised anyway to cover until Hugh gets back on Wednesday.'

'So Nick *is* leaving?' Fiona could feel the blood draining from her face. Had she lost already?

'He's got a flight due to leave at 5 p.m.—if the airport's open, that is.'

Five p.m. The clock had started ticking. The final decision on Fiona's future was only hours away.

Had he been planning to leave without telling her? What on earth was she supposed to say to Sam? He would be building his snowman by now. Elsie had probably found a carrot for a nose and bits of charcoal for the eyes. It would be Uncle Nick that Sam would want to show his creation to.

'I'm sorry, Fi.' Lizzie touched her arm. 'It's none of my business but I can see something's gone wrong. Does it have anything to do with all that rubbish in the paper yesterday?'

'Yeah. Kind of.'

'I can't believe Nick would do something like that.'

'Like what?' Run away to try and escape from a difficult emotional situation? He'd done it before.

'Telling all those things about you. He should know better.'

'He didn't tell. He's as shocked as I was.'

Possibly more. But Lizzie was right. Nick should know better. He should know that running wasn't the answer. That he couldn't escape who he was and he shouldn't want to. It was time he did that final bit of growing up he needed to do.

Or was it just she who could see things so clearly today?

'I'll go and get him, ' she told Lizzie. 'In the Jeep. That will leave Shane here with the ambulance and I'll have my radio if I need to meet him anywhere.'

She was upset.

He could hardly blame her. Lizzie must have told her he was stuck so she'd probably also passed on the news that he was planning to leave today. Right now she was staring at his backpack, propped against the wall behind the milling dogs.

It wasn't something he could have told her over the phone, though. Not when he knew the sound of her voice would be enough to feed the doubts that had grown during the night. Doubts that he was strong enough—unselfish enough—to do the right thing and leave.

Hurting Fiona was the last thing Nick wanted but, seeing her pale face and the rigid way she was holding herself so upright, he knew it was too late. He wanted to hold her. To comfort her. He even took a step forward but Fiona took step away from him and it felt like he was stopped by a solid barrier.

The same barrier that had always been there?

Alistair?

'So…' Fiona bent to pat Tuck and Lass. 'Who's going be looking after these guys?'

'It's only till Wednesday. Hugh was hoping you'd be able to drop by and let them out and feed them.'

'Sure.' Fiona straightened and turned away. 'You ready to go, then?'

No. He wasn't ready but he had no choice. He shouldered his back pack into the rear compartment of the Jeep. He couldn't tell Fiona why he had no choice because he knew what she would say. That she could handle it. That she had lived with ignoring the tabloid press in the past and she could do it again. She wouldn't see that crack between them that was widening. That keeping the legend that was Alistair alive could only increase that chasm.

Fiona was silent, staring ahead as she concentrated on following the tyre tracks she had made on the way in.

'It doesn't have to be for ever, Fi,' Nick said finally. Gently. 'If I go away it'll give you a chance to get Sam's life back on track.'

Fiona snorted. 'You won't come back, Nick. You know that as well as I do. You're running away. It's not as if it's the first time. What's the problem, Nick? Reality chipping away at the fantasy?'

That stung. He wasn't running away to protect himself.

Fiona thought he was.

'Maybe it's time I stopped believing in magic,' he said, more to himself than Fiona. 'Maybe it's time I grew up.'

The Jeep bumped over a frozen rut. 'It's time you grew up all right,' Fiona muttered.

She had every right to be angry but this was unexpected. 'What's that supposed to mean?'

'You have such a chip on your shoulder, Nick. You've got this huge resentment for your brother getting everything *you* wanted. Life is only going to be perfect if you can erase all the bad memories, but have you ever stopped for a moment and considered how bloody lucky you were?'

'What?' They were out of the deep snow now and on the main road but Nick barely noticed the smoother ride.

'Your parents had some strange values,' Fiona said, 'and they screwed up their firstborn son by passing them on. You missed that. You got the chance to discover things for yourself. Important things about what really matters. You wouldn't be the person you are today if you hadn't grown up like that.'

'I should feel lucky that my parents didn't give a damn? That I only got the leftover love that Al didn't need?' Maybe the connection wasn't as strong as he'd believed and Fiona didn't really understand. Bewildered by the attack, Nick was also aware that this was going to make it easier to do what he had to do. He could buy into this argument. It might even be a relief to leave.

'I don't *think* so.'

Fiona ignored the dismissal. 'My past has shaped me as much as yours has shaped you. I'm not going to forget Al, Nick.'

Of course she wasn't going to. No one was. Especially himself.

'Yes, he hurt me,' Fiona continued relentlessly. 'Badly. But I was lucky he came into my life. If I hadn't met him, I wouldn't have met you. We should both be grateful for that.'

Nick frowned. Having been ready to stand his ground, the wind had abruptly been taken out of his sails. She was lucky because she'd met *him*? He should be grateful to Al? That was something he had never considered. He'd been too young when he'd first met Fiona but Al had given them the chance to get to know each other, hadn't he? Had made it possible to see past the barrier that the difference in their ages—or rather, their life experience—had made inevitable. He'd also provided the reason for them to reconnect.

'And I wouldn't have Sam,' Fiona was saying now. Softly. 'He's a part of me, a part of Al and a part of you, too, Nick. He's the past but he's also the future. You don't get a future without a past.'

The radio on the Jeep was crackling as a message came through but Nick was hearing only Fiona's words. It was a novel idea, thanking those that had caused hurt in the past because they'd helped shape the present—and made the future possible.

Was that the way to forgive and forget? Or maybe to accept and forgive. Was there a way forward in this that didn't involve him having to leave behind the woman and child he loved?

'Can you repeat that, please? Message was broken.' Fiona was holding the microphone attached to the dashboard radio. She reached to turn up the volume knob.

They both listened to the address being relayed and the priority dispatch to someone with breathing difficulty.

'But…' Nick was confused. 'Isn't that your address, Fi?'

'Yes.' Fiona flipped a switch and Nick could see the lights from the roof beacons reflecting on the snow drifts lining the road. She pushed another control and the siren began wailing overhead. 'I just hope to God it's not Sam.'

* * *

It wasn't Sam.

Fiona couldn't believe whom she found sitting on the front step of her house, leaning forward and struggling to breathe. She actually stopped halfway along the path that Elsie must have shovelled clear of snow. The heavy, portable oxygen cylinder she was carrying in one hand was forgotten. Weightless.

'You *bastard*!' Nick surged past her. 'What the *hell* do you think you're doing *here*?'

Jeff Smythe was clearly in the grip of a severe asthma attack. His wheeze was clearly audible without a stethoscope. He was breathing at a rate of something more than thirty times a minute and he could only string a couple of words together at a time.

'Want…to apologise…'

'Too late for that,' Nick snapped. He stood, staring down at Jeff, and Fiona could actually see the dramatic change in Nick's features. The control of his fury and the compassion that being a doctor had made intrinsic was appearing, albeit with difficulty. 'Let's get that oxygen on, Fi. You got some salbutamol in this kit?'

'Yes. Of course.' Fiona moved. She set the oxygen cylinder down in the snow and unzipped the side pouch, looking for a nebuliser mask.

Nick flipped open the kit, hunting for the plastic ampoules of the drug that could dilate the airways in Jeff's lungs and make it easier for him to breathe. Elsie was standing behind Jeff, on the veranda of the old villa.

'I told him to go away,' she said anxiously, 'but Sam wanted to show him his snowman.'

Fiona twisted the top off the ampoule and squeezed the contents into the bowl attached to the oxygen mask. She turned on the air flow and vapour began to pour through the mask. She slipped the elastic over Jeff's head. Sam would have done that. Her son found it so easy to trust people. Her gaze landed on the man crouched on the other side of this patient.

So easy to love people. Did Nick have any idea what he was planning to throw away? The trust and love of a small boy? Her head turned towards her mother.

'Where *is* Sam?'

'Inside. Keeping warm. I didn't want the cold to set off *his* asthma.'

'Had this happened before?' Nick asked Jeff.

He nodded.

'Have you used your inhaler?'

'Forgot it.' His voice was muffled by the mask and the hiss of oxygen being released from the cylinder. 'Scared…'

'You'll be all right.' Nick's gaze wasn't as sympathetic as it could have been. He pulled a tourniquet tight on Jeff's arm.

'Had to come…say sorry…Jude won't come…back unless I did…'

'Jude?'

'Girlfriend…'

Fiona dug in the kit and passed Nick what he needed to establish IV access. If this attack didn't respond to the nebulised salbutamol, they would need to administer adrenaline. Intubate Jeff, if it progressed to a respiratory attack. Asthma was not something to be taken lightly. It could be fatal.

'Don't talk,' she instructed Jeff. 'Concentrate on your breathing.'

A snow plough ground its way past the gate with its orange roof light flashing. The red and blue beacons of an ambulance could be seen flashing right beside the plough. The cavalry was arriving.

Jeff was ignoring Fiona's advice. 'Trevor...old friend... visited...last week...'

'And you told him you had a juicy story for him.' Nick sounded disgusted.

'No... Got drunk... Told him Fi-Fiona amazing... Trev got carried away... Thought he was...doing me a favour.'

Fiona was counting the words per breath. Jeff seemed to be finding it just a little easier to speak. She twisted the top off another ampoule and lifted the mask to top up the contents of the bowl.

Nick was taping down the IV cannula. 'So where does Jude fit in to this picture?'

'She read the article...remembered the rally... Wanted to find out how I was doing... We talked all night...'

'Good for you,' Nick said tonelessly. 'You ever been in Intensive Care for your asthma?'

'No.'

'Had a course of prednisone in the past?'

'Not for years.'

'Is this a bad attack for you?'

'Yes.'

'I gave him Sam's inhaler to use,' Elsie said. 'I probably shouldn't have done that, should I?'

'It was good thinking,' Fiona assured her mother. 'For a known asthmatic who uses the same medication, it was the best thing you could have done.'

'It didn't seem to make much difference.'

'Feel better now.' Jeff's rate of breathing was slowing down a little.

Fiona had her fingers on his pulse.

'One-twenty,' she relayed to Nick. 'Down from 140 a couple of minutes ago.'

A movement from the corner of her eye made Fiona turn. Sam was standing on a chair by the window, drawing pictures in the condensation.

Shane was coming up the path. He had Lizzie following.

'We thought it was Sam having the asthma attack,' Lizzie said. 'Good heavens, I've seen you before.' She stared at Jeff. 'You're the man who lost his finger, aren't you?'

'You're that journalist,' Shane added. 'I'll bet you had something to do with that trashy stuff in the paper yesterday. You bastard!'

'I'm sorry…' Jeff was looking up at Fiona. 'I'm really sorry. Trevor's a loose cannon but…I can make sure nothing else gets printed.'

'You'd better,' Nick growled.

Jeff was definitely breathing far more easily. The danger had passed but he was going to need observation for a while yet.

'Take him down to the hospital,' Fiona told Shane. 'Lizzie, can you travel with him, please? Keep up the nebulised salbutamol. We'll follow in the Jeep.'

'Sure.' Shane and Lizzie went to get the stretcher.

A tapping on the window caught Nick's attention. Sam had rubbed enough of a clear space to see what was going on outside. He was waving happily. Nick waved back.

The stretcher was being pushed down the path when the small figure appeared from behind Elsie.

'Uncle Nick, did you see my snowman?'

'Not yet, buddy.'

'It's just there. *See?*'

Fiona looked, too. Three stacked balls of snow.

Branches poked at drunken angles for arms. A carrot nose and stones made a lopsided, smiling mouth. Camellia leaves with nice, sturdy stems had been poked into the head to make glossy, green hair.

'It's the best snowman I've ever seen,' Nick told Sam as Shane and Lizzie propelled the stretcher bearing Jeff back towards the gate. Then he caught Fiona's gaze and lowered his voice to a murmur only audible to her. 'Almost.'

And Fiona was propelled back in time. Back to the time and place she had realised how special Nick was. When they'd had that snowball fight and made their own snowman.

When she'd begun to love this man.

Had that been when Nick had fallen in love with her?

That's what the message in his gaze appeared to be. Fiona couldn't look away. So much had happened since then. They were different people but the love was still there, wasn't it?

She could see it.

Feel it.

Fiona still couldn't look away. Not until she heard the sound of the back doors of the ambulance slamming shut. And then Shane's voice.

'You two coming, or what?'

It took a couple of minutes for Shane to manoeuvre the heavy ambulance in a U-turn in the narrow space the plough had cleared. Fiona and Nick sat in the Jeep, waiting to follow.

Holding hands…

'You're right,' Nick said quietly. 'I *am* lucky. I *should* thank my parents. And Al. *Especially* Al, because he found you.'

'I'm not chasing a ghost, Nick. If that's all I'd seen in you, I would have run a country mile.'

'You wouldn't have taken me home? Let me meet Sam?'

'I might have done that,' Fiona conceded, 'but I certainly wouldn't have fallen in love with you, Nick. Your connection to Al and his world would have been enough to put me right off.'

'It hasn't been? Even after yesterday?'

'I did a lot of thinking last night.' Fiona held more tightly to Nick's hand. 'Yesterday was shocking because it made me remember just how much I hated that world and everything in it.'

'You hated Al?'

'For a while. Not any more. He was a product of that world and he needed to be part of it to survive. I don't and I don't want Sam to need it but, at some point, he's going to have to make his own choices. I was just burying my head in the sand to think I could keep it completely out of my life.'

'But you did—until I turned up.'

'Yes. And I could have continued to do that. Maybe I would have, if the pull hadn't been so strong.' Fiona swallowed. 'I love you Nick. I want to be with you. Not because of who your brother was.' She held his gaze. '*In spite* of it. We belong together. You and me and Sam…' Fiona's eyes filled with tears, which made Nick all blurry. 'Together,' she finished with a wobble in her voice.

'For ever?' The word was a whisper of hope and a promise, all in one.

Fiona nodded and the tears spilled over. 'For ever.'

And then Nick was holding her face, his fingers brushing the tears away. Then his lips were on her forehead, her closed eyelids…her lips.

'You were right about something else, too,' he murmured.

'What's that?' Fiona's voice was still shaky.

'Magic happens.'

The honk from the air horn of the ambulance was an intrusion. Shane's grinning face as he drove past indicated approval for what was going on in the Jeep. His thumbs-up made them both smile.

'We should go,' Fiona said reluctantly. 'We've got a patient in there that we abandoned.'

'He's getting all the care he needs. Probably more than he deserves.' But Nick was still smiling as Fiona slipped the vehicle into gear and pulled away. 'Poor devil. He fell in love with you. Can't really blame him for that, can I?'

'He'll be all right. He's moved on already. Or moved back.'

Nick's hand was on the side of Fiona's face. A gentle touch that made her want to cry again.

'Have we moved on, hon? Or back?'

'We've just moved.' Fiona could feel the misery of the last twenty-four hours vanishing, along with any doubts she had harboured. 'Sideways, maybe. We've got to the place we need to be, that's all that matters. The place we belong.'

'For ever,' Nick added firmly. It wasn't a question but Fiona answered anyway.

'You bet it's for ever. I love you so much, Nick.'

'I love you, too.' Nick's voice had the ring of assurance. The kind of happiness Fiona was allowing to envelop her. 'Always have, always will.'

CHAPTER TWELVE

THE opening of Lakeview's purpose-built, state-of-the-art ambulance station was a grand occasion.

A large crowd had turned out under the clear blue skies of a late Central Otago summer, nearly two years after Nick Stewart had arrived in New Zealand.

Maggie Patterson had the honour of cutting the wide red ribbon strung across the open doors of the large garage. Her proud husband—the medical director of Lakeview Hospital—was standing beside her and a huge cheer went up from the watching crowd as the ribbon parted and fell to make a silken river on the black asphalt.

Fiona Stewart leaned closer to the man standing beside her at the front of the audience.

Her husband.

Nick put his arm around her. 'You should have been up there, helping to cut that ribbon.'

Fiona laughed. She patted the impressive mound of her tummy. 'There isn't a uniform in creation that would fit me at the moment. I think they've got it wrong, you know. I'm sure there must be at least twins hiding in there.'

'If there is, we might have to send back that lovely new

scanner we got from the extra funding. It would be seriously faulty.'

Hugh had turned to face the crowd. Someone handed him a microphone. 'Nobody's feeling sick out there in this heat, are they?' he inquired hopefully. 'Because we've got some fabulous new gear we wouldn't mind playing with.'

A ripple of laughter went through the audience. Nick had his mouth close to Fiona's ear.

'You're not missing it too much, are you? Being on active duty?'

'Are you kidding? We've had a fabulous time overseas, we've just had the foundation poured for the house of our dreams and our daughter's due to put in an appearance any day now. I might never want to go back to work. Ooh…' Fiona's face scrunched into lines of discomfort.

'What's the matter?'

'This baby has a kick like a mule. Feel that!' Taking Nick's hand in hers, Fiona laid it on her belly—a contact that they had become expert in. She was watching his face as their baby moved again. She loved that look of incredulity that never seemed to fade no matter how often he felt it. And the look of dreamy contentment that invariably followed.

'Mummy, we want to go and play on the bouncy castle.' Sam was six now and shooting up. His friend Luke was beside him as usual and the two boys were clearly bored with the formal proceedings of the day. The entertainment and food that was being laid on after the speeches were of far greater appeal.

'Shh,' Fiona warned. 'Uncle Hugh's still talking.'

'We have so many people to thank,' Hugh was saying. 'Everybody in this community has been involved in some way, helping to get us to this point. I hope it's just a good insurance policy but if you need us, we'll be there for you. All of you.'

Nick still hand his hand resting protectively on Fiona's belly. 'I'm here for you,' he said in a stage whisper. 'All of you.'

Fiona giggled. 'There's quite a lot of me at the moment.' She took a glance over her shoulder. He didn't mean just her and the precious extra family member she was carrying, though, did he?

Elsie was standing behind them. Her wedding ring glinted in the sun as she reached out to distract Sam who was playing 'paper, scissors, rock' with Luke and had just thumped his friend's 'scissors' with his 'rock'. Then she leaned back into the position she was so often in, close enough to touch Bernie.

Bernie was holding Luke's little sister, Lucy, and seemed to be thoroughly enjoying his role of de facto grandfather for the youngest member of the Patterson household. Lucy was ignoring the sound of her father's voice as he continued with his speech, intent on removing Bernie's sunglasses.

Fiona hadn't heard the last thing Hugh had said but it had created a spontaneous round of applause. A photographer walked closer to get a better shot and the man following in his wake was scribbling busily in a notebook. He held his pen slightly oddly but you had to look closely to see that he had a finger missing.

Jeff had done them all proud in the long fundraising campaign that had led to this celebration, putting in countless unpaid hours of effort.

'I owe you guys,' was all he'd said whenever anybody had tried to thank him. 'Big time.'

Jeff's wife Jude would be somewhere in this crowd,

Fiona realised. She would have to find her later and see how she was keeping in the early stages of *her* pregnancy.

'In a minute we're going to invite you all to look inside,' Hugh said. 'Take a look at the office, the sleeping accommodation that means we now have trained staff available twenty-four seven and meet some of our new permanent staff members who will be only too delighted to show you some of the new equipment. You might be lucky and get a free blood-pressure check or even an ECG.'

'I might get lucky and get to sit down,' Fiona whispered to Nick. 'My back's killing me.'

'Come and sit down now. Somewhere shady.'

Fiona shook her head. 'Hugh's almost finished. I don't want to attract attention.'

Hugh couldn't possibly have heard her. He certainly wouldn't have changed what he was about to say, anyway.

'While I'm here, it's a great opportunity to introduce the newest member of our hospital staff. Recently back from post-grad training overseas, we're lucky enough to have persuaded Dr Nick Stewart to become our resident surgeon. Nick? Where are you?'

There had been a time when both Nick and Fiona would have shied away from such public scrutiny. Taken steps to avoid the camera lens that was swinging in their direction.

But now they just stood there. Holding hands and smiling. First for the camera and then for each other, as the applause around them became the background for another cheer.

Fiona's smile faded, however. It became a grimace.

'Nick?'

'Yes, hon?'

'You know what you said about sitting down?'

'Let's go.' Nick was supporting her firmly but Fiona couldn't move.

'It's hurting too much,' she groaned. 'Oh, help. I think I'm in labour, Nick.'

Hugh was still watching them but his eyebrows were raised. He could see something might be amiss. He strode in their direction, with Maggie right behind him.

'Got one of those fancy new stretchers from the new ambulance in there, Maggie?'

'Sure.' Maggie was looking intently at Fiona's face. 'Uh-oh!'

'I know.' Fiona tried to take a new breath. How could contractions start this suddenly and with such ferocity? 'Good timing, isn't it?'

'Let's go and get that stretcher,' Hugh said. He pulled Maggie's arm. 'Today might be good.'

'I reckon.' But Nick was grinning. 'I know we've advertised entertainment for everybody this afternoon but I think I'd rather our baby got born inside.'

And so she was.

Charlotte Jane Murchison Stewart was born a mere thirty minutes later, in the relative privacy of Lakeview's emergency department.

The small crowd of family and friends in the waiting room had been quite content to miss the start of the festivities outside.

Except for Sam. He gave up waiting patiently and sneaked into the room his mother had disappeared into.

'Dad?'

'Over here, buddy.'

Sam stared at the tiny face in the bundle Nick was holding. 'Is that it?'

'That's your sister,' Fiona told him. 'Isn't she gorgeous?'

'Yeah…I guess. Can I go and get an ice cream now?'

'In a minute.' Nick was handing something to Hugh, who had been supervising a very straightforward birth. 'Do you mind, mate?'

'Not at all.'

Nick placed the bundle that was Charlotte into Fiona's arms with infinite care. Then he scooped Sam up with one arm, making him squeak with glee, before perching on the side of the bed, one arm across the pillow to encircle his wife and baby, the other holding Sam securely on his knee.

'A family photo,' Nick declared. 'The first of many.'

Fiona tilted her head, tearing her gaze away from her newborn to bask in the love she could see in her husband's gaze. Sam chose that moment to reach out and see if that fluff on his new sister's head was as soft as it looked.

And the camera shutter clicked, capturing a tiny circle linked by touch and so much more.

By love. By a future they would all share.

As a family.

MILLS & BOON
MEDICAL
On sale 4th July 2008

VIRGIN MIDWIFE, PLAYBOY DOCTOR
by Margaret McDonagh

BRIDES OF PENHALLY BAY
Bachelor doctors become husbands and fathers –
in a place where hearts are made whole

Oliver Fawkner is new to Penhally Bay – and this seriously sexy doctor, with a playboy reputation, has caused quite a stir with the female population! However, Oliver only seems interested in getting to know beautiful, innocent midwife Chloe MacKinnon…

THE REBEL DOCTOR'S BRIDE
by Sarah Morgan

Sexy but dangerous! That's how the residents of Glenmore Island remember Conner MacNeil. Now he's back – and although he's a top-notch surgeon, the twinkle in his eye promises he's as rebellious as ever. It's going to take every ounce of his charm to win over his patients – *and* his practice nurse, Flora Harris…

THE SURGEON'S SECRET BABY WISH
by Laura Iding

Paediatrician Naomi Horton longs to have a baby of her own. Only her gorgeous new boss Rick Weber suddenly makes Naomi realise she wants a loving husband too. If only a family were on Nick's agenda…

Queens of Romance

Impulse

Rebecca Malone sold all her possessions and jumped on a
plane to Corfu! So when sexy stranger Stephen Nikodemus
began to romance her, all she had to do was enjoy it…

The Best Mistake

Zoe Fleming was a hardworking single mum looking for a
tenant, not a lover, a father for her son or a husband. Then
sexy, single, gorgeous J Cooper McKinnon turned up!

Temptation

When socialite Eden Carlborough came crashing down from
one of his apple trees into his arms, wealthy bachelor Chase
Elliot knew she was simply too delicious to resist.

Available 4th July 2008

Collect all 10 superb books in the collection!

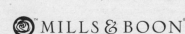

FREE!
4 Books
and a surprise gift!

We would like to take this opportunity to thank you for reading this Mills & Boon® book by offering you the chance to take FOUR more specially selected titles from the Medical™ series absolutely FREE! We're also making this offer to introduce you to the benefits of the Mills & Boon® Reader Service™—

- ★ **FREE home delivery**
- ★ **FREE gifts and competitions**
- ★ **FREE monthly Newsletter**
- ★ **Exclusive Reader Service offers**
- ★ **Books available before they're in the shops**

Accepting these FREE books and gift places you under no obligation to buy, you may cancel at any time, even after receiving your free shipment. Simply complete your details below and return the entire page to the address below. You don't even need a stamp!

YES! Please send me 4 free Medical books and a surprise gift. I understand that unless you hear from me, I will receive 6 superb new titles every month for just £2.99 each, postage and packing free. I am under no obligation to purchase any books and may cancel my subscription at any time. The free books and gift will be mine to keep in any case.

M8ZEF

Ms/Mrs/Miss/Mr ....Initials ....
BLOCK CAPITALS PLEASE

Surname ....

Address...

....

....Postcode ....

Send this whole page to:
UK: FREEPOST CN81, Croydon, CR9 3WZ